I0570939

The Willies Chronicles

Witch in the Woods

C.S. Curtis

Copyright © 2012 C.S. Curtis

All rights reserved.

Hardback
ISBN: 12984134
ISBN-13: 978-1-105-88225-8

Paperback
ISBN: 0615658318
ISBN-13: 978-0615658315

DEDICATION

To my dear family and friends who believed in me and have encouraged me, whether by words or a swift kick in the rear.

And to all the Willies who see what only Willies can see.

CONTENTS

1

Pinky Swear

J ason could hear his heart pounding in his ears. His lungs burned in his chest as he pushed himself to run as fast as his small feet would carry him. Unlike most trips down the rarely used dirt road, this time he took no notice of the patterns made by his shoes as they pressed into the dusty wheel ruts. Part of him wanted to look back over his shoulder to see what was behind him, but the rest of Jason wanted to keep on running and never look back.

"Where's that stump?" he thought, as he looked for the moss-covered tree stump that marked a small trail that acted as a shortcut through a grove of low hanging trees. He began to panic as he feared he had missed the turn off and would have to take the long way home. Suddenly the landmark stump came into view and Jason veered off the dirt road and onto the narrow trail. Feather-soft ferns brushed against his bare legs as he wound his way along the trail. Dead branches, hanging just a few feet above the ground, raked across Jason's scalp as he fought to keep up his pace.

Breaking through some low hanging branches Jason stumbled into the backyard of his home nearly flattening a ten-year-old girl with a mane of wavy brown hair.

"Hey watch it squirt!" Jessica yelled at her brother. "You act like you just saw a ghost."

"Worse," Jason panted.

"Worse than a ghost? What's worse than a ghost? A cyclops? An ogre? The ghost of an ogre?" his sister teased.

Jason bent over with his hands on his knees as he caught his breath. Then looking back at the shortcut in fear he added, "A witch!"

"What?"

"I saw her!" he yelled. Beads of sweat trailed from his spiky blonde hair, down through the thin layer of dirt coating his face. His eyes widened in excitement as he again peered back at the still swaying branches he had just burst through. "It was the Witch of Redwood Glen!"

"You saw her? Honest to goodness?" Jessica said as her hazel eyes danced with excitement. "Where was she?"

"Up at Wexler's Pond."

"Wexler's Pond? Are you crazy? You aren't supposed to go past the end of the short cut. Boy are you gonna get it when Mom finds out."

"You aren't gonna tell her are you?"

"What's going to stop me? You're just a little six-year-old kid Jace. You can't go running off anywhere you want."

"But you know what's gonna happen if you tell her I went up the dirt road," he pleaded.

"Yep, but maybe if you get in trouble for it this time you won't do it again."

"But if you tell Mom where I went, she's gonna wanna know why you weren't watching me," Jason pointed out.

"The kid's right," Jessica reasoned to herself. "Ratting out the squirt will only get me in trouble too. With my luck I'll probably get the worst of it."

"I tell you what I'm going do," Jessica said to her little brother. "Because I don't want to see you in trouble, I won't tell Mom—this time."

"Promise?" Jason asked.

"Promise. Of course, if you ever take off on your own like that again the deal is off."

"It's a deal!" Jason said excitedly. "Pinky swear?"

"Oh, all right," Jessica conceded as she extended her pinky to her brother. "I pinky swear."

"I pinky swear," Jason agreed.

"So what exactly did you see?" Jessica asked.

Jason looked anxiously back at the shortcut to the dirt road as if something would leap out of it at any moment. Then lowering his voice he whispered, "I saw the witch. Just like the kids at school described her."

"With the stringy white hair?" Jessica whispered back. "And the big nose?"

"Well I couldn't see her nose, but she had the stringy white hair for sure."

"What was she doing?"

"She was sitting on the log where we roasted some mores on July fourth."

"S'mores," Jessica corrected him.

"Some more what?" Jason asked.

"Not some more. They're called s'mores."

"Oh. I always thought they were named some mores because I always want some more."

"Forget the s'mores," Jessica said in exasperation. "Get on with what you saw."

"Well she was sitting there holding something in her lap. I sneaked through the bushes as close as I could get, and I think she was holding a jack rabbit."

"I wonder what she was doing with it," Jessica pondered.

"I think she was probably gonna do a magic spell with it."

"That's silly Jason. There is no such thing as magic."

"Is too," Jason argued.

"Is not," she insisted.

"Is!"

"Isn't!"

Jason was about to respond again when he felt a tap on his left shoulder. As he looked to his left shoulder he saw a skeleton's hand resting on his shoulder. Letting out a blood-curdling scream, he jumped to his right and suddenly the whole world went black.

2

Like a Kick in the Head

J ason's eyes fluttered open for a moment, and then he squeezed them shut. He knew he must be dead. In the brief time he had them open, he had seen an angel.

"That is what they talk about when you die. You see a bright light and angels," he thought, as the image he had just seen lingered in his eyes. There had been a fuzzy-looking angel face with a bright glow like a halo around it. And it had all been so bright. Even his body seemed different. He felt like he was almost floating. He could tell he wasn't on the ground, but he also wasn't standing up.

"Jason, Jason," his mother's tender voice reached his ears.

"I'm going to be all right Mom," he mumbled. "You and Jessica will be okay without me."

"What are you talking about Jason?" his mother asked.

"I see the light Mom, the angels are here to get me," Jason murmured as if in a dream.

"You dummy. You only whacked your head on a tree branch Jason. You ain't dead," Jessica interjected.

"Aren't Jessica, not ain't," her mother corrected. "And don't call anyone dummy."

"Sorry Mom," Jessica said meekly.

Jason opened his eyes, and his vision focused on his mother's face. His grandmother always said Jessica was the spitting image of his mother when she was Jessica's age. He always wondered how his grandmother could compare his beautiful mother with his goofy-looking sister. Looking up at his mother, he could clearly see concern crease her brow as she looked down at her youngest child. His mother knelt on the ground and cradled his body softly in her arms.

"I thought the witch had finished me off for sure."

"Witch? What are you talking about?" his mother asked.

"Um, well, I saw these really bony fingers on my shoulder, and I figured that only a witch could have fingers like that."

Laughing lightly at the image Jason presented, his mother explained, "That was a section of a demonstration skeleton I borrowed from school to study for my anatomy exam. I just thought it would make you jump. I didn't think you would get hurt. I'm so sorry honey."

"It's okay Mom."

"Thank you. I think you're going to be all right Jason. But I'm afraid you're going to have a nasty knot on your forehead," his mother consoled him.

It wasn't until his mother mentioned his forehead that he felt the throbbing pain from the right side of his forehead. The knot seemed to pulsate, and the pain was spreading over the top of his head.

"Ow," he exclaimed as he touched the reddening bump for the first time.

"Don't touch it honey. I'll make an ice pack and give you something to help with the pain," his mother promised as she helped him to his feet. "Come along inside and we'll take care of you."

Jason dutifully followed his mother into the house but paused at the back door and turned to Jessica. In crude pantomime, he motioned to his older sister that he still wanted to talk to her about the witch he saw. Nodding to Jason, she signaled that she would be in to get the whole story from him. Fifteen minutes of hugs from Dr. Mom and an ice pack later found Jason reclining on his bed sipping juice through a bendy straw.

"Looks like you have it made," Jessica said as she plopped down at the foot of her brother's bed. "All it takes is a little bump on the noggin and you even get juice in bed."

"Little bump?" Jason said, feeling a bit hurt by the comment. "It's amazing I'm still alive. That tree could have knocked my head off."

"Tree? You hit a little branch not much bigger than my thumb. And even then your head hurt the branch more than it hurt you."

"That's not true. That thing was massive. It had to be to make this thing," he said, jabbing his thumb at his forehead.

"Well, you can probably see the twig from your window," Jessica offered defensively. Peering out the window that paralleled the side of Jason's bed she scanned the backyard for where her brother's accident had happened. "There," she said, pointing to the left of an Adirondack chair. "There is where it happened. See where the path is to the left of the chair?"

"Ok, I see it. And that tree branch is pretty big. So I'm right."

"But that isn't the branch you hit," Jessica countered. "The branch you hit was a smaller one coming off of that one. If you look on the ground, you can see the part that broke off when your head hit it."

Gazing at the ground beneath the larger branch, he saw a small pile of slender branches. The impact had broken the old dry wood into several small sections.

"Well it sure felt a lot bigger than it looks," Jason softly conceded. "In fact, it hurts just looking at it."

"I'll admit you did a pretty good job of destroying that branch," Jessica said with a light laugh. "You could probably make good money using your head to make firewood out of branches."

"Ha, ha. That was so funny, not!" Jason scoffed. "Well, you could make money by using your..." his voice trailed off.

"Can't think of a comeback huh?"

"What's that?" Jason said pointing to the bushes where the shortcut started at the edge of the backyard.

Jessica craned her neck to get a better look, "Is it a cat? Or maybe a skunk."

"It doesn't seem to have fur," Jason whispered. "I'm getting a creepy feeling about that thing."

3

Hollow Eyes

Peering out of the bushes was an animal about three feet tall. It was partially hidden by the bushes, but it appeared to be standing on two legs. The creature seemed to be checking to see if anyone was in the yard, and then it crept out of the bushes. Both children gasped as they got a better view of the animal. Jason had been right that it had no fur—the only hair was on the tips of the sharply pointed ears and a small patch on the top of its head. The creature resembled a thin, spindly dwarf but moved like an animal more than a human. A thin, reddish skin stretched over its body and made it easier to see that the legs bent backwards like a goat's and ended in small pointed hooves. The gaze of the creature was fixed on the ground so the children were unable to see its face.

Squatting over the small pile of broken branch pieces, the animal appeared to study the pieces of wood. Thin, tentacle-like, fingers reached out and wrapped around one piece of wood. With its head still bowed, it drew the twig to its face and appeared to be closely examining the wood. It seemed to smell the wood intently, and then a tongue that would be well-suited for a large snake flicked out and ran along the surface of the wood.

The creature once again looked carefully around the yard. Then it scanned the back of the small house. This let the children get a better look at the face of the animal. There was no readily recognizable nose, though there did appear to be nostril slits in the middle of its face. The mouth jutted out

11

slightly like a snub-nosed lizard. As its gaze reached Jason's window the children froze. The eyes were deep set, and chills ran down the spines of both children as they sensed emptiness in the eyes, as if there was nothing inside the creature itself. The eyes, those deep, hollow eyes, fixed on Jessica. While one eye stayed fixed on the girl, the other continued to scan and stopped when it discovered Jason's face.

At first the children felt frozen in place. Perhaps it was fear of being noticed if they moved. When they saw a small plume of smoke rising from the stick in the creatures hand Jason's jaw dropped. Sensing the motion in the window the creature bared a set of jagged fangs and the hollow eyes seemed to widen.

In a split second, the short creature collapsed into a small pile of red skin. It wriggled in place for a moment and then started slithering back towards the bushes. It no longer appeared as a small two-legged animal. Now it resembled a short fat snake. Just before the squirming red snake-like creature reached the safety of the bushes a large Red-Tailed Hawk swooped down and grasped its writhing body. Before the children could react to the sudden appearance of the bird, it had disappeared over the trees.

"What was that?" Jason finally managed to whisper.

"I think it was a hawk," Jessica whispered back, equally entranced by what they had just seen.

"Not the bird. I mean what was that thing we saw? That weird red thing that came through the bushes."

"Well, the bird flew off with a red snake," Jessica whispered. "But whatever was there before the snake, I have no idea. I've never seen anything like it."

"Me neither," Jason said in awe. "Do you think she sent it?"

"She?"

"The witch," Jason whispered. "I think she made that thing and sent it to find me."

"You're nuts," Jessica accused.

"Or maybe it was the witch! Maybe she turned herself into that thing."

"Nuts!"

"Am not."

"Are too. Everyone knows there are no such things as witches."

"Well I saw her."

"Just because you saw some old lady doesn't make her a witch," argued Jessica.

"Well she looked like one. And I think she is the reason that thing was out there in the yard."

"You're a nut," Jessica insisted as she left Jason staring out his window at the spot where the red creature had appeared.

"Am not," he muttered under his breath.

"Are too," came the response as his sister disappeared down the hallway.

After studying the backyard from his vantage point for a few minutes more, Jason finally lay down and stared at his ceiling.

Feeling his head throb with pain, he gingerly touched the goose egg that had formed on his forehead.

"I wish this thing would go away," he said softly. "It makes my whole body hurt."

Sleep soon overtook the exhausted boy, and he slept deeply through dinnertime and into the night.

4

A Big Surprise

J ason woke with a start, as the early morning sunlight found a gap in his bedroom curtains and splashed across his face. While his sleep had been deep, it was also marked by vivid dreams containing little red creatures, hawks, and witches. The dreams were little more than a replay of what he had witnessed the day before from his bedroom window. In some, the scene was repeated as he had seen it. In others, the witch came through the bushes instead of the red creature. Still another dream had the witch coming through the bushes before she turned into the little red creature. While it had at first startled him, the sun on his face was actually a relief to Jason as he realized night was over and so were his dreams.

Sitting up in bed, he leaned toward the gap in his curtains and peered with one eye out into the backyard. He half expected to see the red creature standing in the same spot it was the day before. Jason let out a sigh of relief as he noticed the only thing moving in the yard was a grey squirrel scampering across the lawn. Pulling the curtains tightly together, he was able to keep the stream of sunlight out of his room and block his view of where the creature had been. In truth, he was really trying to keep the creature from seeing him.

Changing into shorts and a T-shirt, Jason readied himself for the day. Grabbing a handful of small objects from the top of his dresser, he shoved them into the pockets of his shorts and headed downstairs for breakfast. Jessica sat at the kitchen table reading a book as she absent-mindedly stabbed her spoon into a bowl of cereal. Wendy Cowell stood at the kitchen sink, rinsing dishes and stacking them on the counter.

"Morning Mom," Jason said as he entered the room.

"Good morning honey. How are you feeling?" his mother responded, without turning around.

"Better," he responded as he plopped into his usual chair at the table. "Whatcha doing Jess?"

"What's it look like I'm doing?" his sister snorted in reply without taking her eyes off the page. "How's that lump of a head of yours doing?"

"Now Jessica," his mother scolded as she brought Jason a bowl of cereal. "Be nice to your brother. He got a nasty lump on his head and it will take time to heal."

Setting the bowl before Jason, his mother gently tilted his head up so she could get a good look at his forehead.

"Oh Jason!" she said in shock.

"What is it?" Jessica said looking up from her book. "Oh wow!"

"What?" Jason said in concern. "What's wrong?"

"It's your forehead honey."

"Does it look really bad?"

"It doesn't look like anything," Jessica said in awe.

"Not a mark on you dear," his mother said as she tilted his head back and forth in the light to see if she might be missing some swelling. "It's amazing. No swelling, no discoloration, not a single scratch on you."

"Really?" Jason said doubtfully as he reached up and gingerly touched his forehead. Feeling no pain, he ran his hand across his brow seeking a bump. "Wow, it's just like I wished for last night."

"What is that dear?" asked his mother.

"Well, before I went to sleep, I wished that the pain and the bump would go away and it did."

"Well I think it's wonderful," his mother added.

"I think it's weird," Jessica mumbled as she returned to her book and cereal. As Jason dug into his bowl of cereal he couldn't help but notice Jessica periodically glancing at his forehead and then quickly back to her book.

When their Mom left the room for a few minutes, Jessica spoke softly to her brother, "Mom has to go over to the college for the morning. How would you like to try and track down that weird red thing we saw yesterday?"

"Cool," he whispered back. "Maybe we can catch it."

"I'm afraid of what it would do if we tried."

"It was so weird looking," Jason said.

"What was so weird looking?" his mother said as she reentered the room.

"His forehead," Jessica said thinking quickly. "His forehead was really weird looking yesterday and poof! Just look at it now."

"Well, I think he looks adorable with or without the lump," his mother said, bending down to kiss his forehead.

"Aw Mom," Jason said wiping the kiss from his forehead.

18

"Oh, you're so adorable," Jessica teased as she leaned over and pinched her brother's cheek.

"Cut it out," Jason pleaded.

"Now Jess," her mother said seriously. "You're going to be in charge while I'm at school. And that means you need to look after your brother, not annoy him."

"Yes Mom," she agreed.

"What do you two think you'll do while I'm gone?"

Jason opened up his mouth to speak when Jessica cut him off, "We're thinking we might go for a hike up the dirt road."

"That sounds like fun," their mother said cheerfully. "Just remember the rule. Always…"

"Stick together," Jason finished the sentence.

"We know Mom," Jessica reassured her mother. "Don't worry, we're only going for a hike."

Fortunately for Jessica, her mother was already busy gathering up her book bag and purse and hadn't given her full attention to what her daughter had said.

"Well good, kids. Stay safe and don't go too far. It looks like it's a perfect day for a hike. If you need me just call my cell phone."

"Ok Mom," Jessica replied.

"Oh, and Jess you'll need to make lunch."

"Ok Mom."

"I'll be back in time to make dinner."

"Ok Mom," Jessica said wearily.

"And one more thing," their mother said, pausing at the back door.

"What's that?" Jessica asked.

"Don't let bony witch hands get you," she said as she winked at Jason. Then blowing her children kisses, she rushed off to her car.

"I thought she would never leave," Jessica said with a note of exasperation in her voice. Taking her cereal bowl to the kitchen sink, she rinsed it and placed it with the other dishes her mother had rinsed.

"I can't believe you lied to Mom."

"What do you mean?" Jessica asked.

"You told Mom we're going on a hike, not that we're going to track that creature."

"Don't you think tracking that thing will involve a little bit of hiking?"

"Well, yeah."

"And I told her we'd be going on the dirt road right?"

"Right."

"Since that thing came out from the trail that leads to that road, we'll probably end up on the dirt road. So I didn't lie to Mom at all. We will be hiking and we will be on that road. I just didn't mention anything about the creature."

"Oh," Jason said. "So it wasn't a lie?"

"Nope. Not a lie at all..." her voice trailed off and she dropped her bowl on the counter. The bowl hit hard but didn't break. It wobbled uneasily for a moment and finally settled onto the counter.

"Jason," she hissed lowly at her brother. "I think that thing is back."

5

Hunting the Creature

"J ason," Jessica hissed again more intently.

"I'm right here," he whispered at her elbow. His speed at getting to her side surprised Jessica and she jumped slightly. "Where is it?"

"Don't sneak up on me like that," Jessica said angrily as she felt her heart race. "It's over by the garden shed."

"Where? I can't see?" Jason stretched to see over the sill of the window that was set above the sink. Jessica helped her brother pull himself up onto the counter to look out the window.

"It's right over there," Jessica whispered as she pointed to the right side of the small garden shed. "Well, it was there a minute ago."

The siblings scanned the side yard trying to spot the creature.

"I wonder if it went back to where it came out of the trees yesterday," Jessica theorized.

Jason hopped down from the counter, and the two went down the hallway to the back door. The pair crept up cautiously to the back door and gazed out the window. Their gaze first settled on the area they had seen the creature the day before, but there was no sign of its little red body. Suddenly Jason gasped. Jessica dropped her eyes from the backyard to look down on the steps leading to the back porch and she saw what had made her brother react. The little red creature was standing on the steps to the porch. It was bent over and seemed to be picking at the base of the porch railing. Plucking a leaf that was stuck between two rails, the creature sniffed it and gave the leaf a lick.

"I don't think it's the same one we saw yesterday," Jessica whispered softly.

"What do you mean?"

"The other one had a rounder head. This one's head seems a bit pointy."

"Are you sure?" Jason whispered a bit louder.

Apparently the creature heard Jason's voice because it suddenly turned and stared straight at the siblings. Like the round-headed creature they had seen the day before, this one had dark hollow-looking eyes that almost seemed to look straight through them. Baring sharp little fangs, it made a loud hiss at the children before scampering into a bush at the base of the steps. A moment later, a fat red snake slithered out of the bush and started moving across the back lawn. It paused several feet away from the porch steps and coiled up. Raising its head, it looked back and hissed at the startled children. Then the snake slid quickly into the brush at the far edge of the lawn. As the tip of its tail disappeared under a fern, three large red-tailed hawks landed on the lawn.

"There are more hawks this time," Jessica said softly. "Remember a hawk showed up yesterday and took off with the snake?"

"The hawks hunt the snakes."

"Call me crazy but I think the snakes are the little red creatures. Each time we saw a creature it disappeared, and then we saw a snake."

"You're crazy. But I think you're right."

"Then why did you call me crazy?"

"You said I could. How often do I get a chance like that?" Jason chuckled. For the first time since Jessica saw the creature from the kitchen window, the children felt they could relax.

The siblings watched as the birds hopped across the lawn toward the fern the snake had slid under. They seemed to be working together to hunt the snake.

"It looks kind of like they're talking to each other," Jessica said as the birds would move their beaks and nod their heads at each other. One of the hawks moved cautiously into the fern and disappeared from the view of the children. After a minute or two the hawk returned to other two. Once again it appeared that the birds were discussing something. This time, however, the birds were glancing and nodding towards the back of the house.

"What do you think hawks would say to each other?" Jason wondered out loud.

"Who knows," Jessica answered absently. "But I kind of wonder what they would talk about if they could talk."

"Didn't I just say that?"

"Say what?" Jessica asked.

"Never mind," Jason muttered as they watched the hawks take to the air. One hawk flew up and over the trees that separated the children's back yard from the old dirt road. The other hawks flew up and over the house and out of sight of their human audience. The children lingered at the window for several more minutes, waiting to see if there would be any more activity.

"You ready to go hunting?" Jessica asked her little brother.

"You still want to?"

"Yep," she said confidently. "We even have a fresh trail now."

"Let me get my shoes on then," Jason said as he hurried off to grab his shoes. Jessica busied herself in the kitchen while waiting for her brother. When he returned, she held up her school backpack.

"Snacks for the hunt, er, the hike," she said with a smile that was a carbon copy of their mother's. The children stepped out onto the back porch, and Jessica locked the door behind them.

"Let's start over by the fern where the hawks and snake went," Jessica suggested.

"What should we look for?"

"Any kind of track that looks like a snake made it. And keep an eye out for any kind of mark in the dirt that looks like it could have been made by those little red things."

"Ok," Jason agreed as they walked down the steps of the porch. He paused before stepping off the last step. His eyes studied the bush they had seen the creature go into and where the red snake had come out. He half expected those hollow eyes to be looking back at him from inside the bush.

"What are you doing Jace?"

"I just wanted to make sure that thing wasn't still in there."

"What do you see?"

"A bush."

"Let's keep going then," Jessica said, and led her brother across the back lawn. Periodically she would stop and take a good look at a bare patch of ground hoping to see marks made by what they were tracking. Slowly scanning for tracks the children finally arrived at the fern on the edge of the lawn. But what they encountered there made them retreat to the middle of the lawn.

6

Small Tracks and Big Stinks

"Eww, gross!" Jason said as he pinched his nostrils closed. "That stinks. Was that you?"

"That wasn't me," Jessica defended herself as she too pinched her nostrils closed. "It doesn't even smell human."

"Human? It doesn't smell animal."

"It smells worse than anything I have ever smelled," Jessica complained. "It does remind me of something I have smelled before."

"What was that?"

"I can't remember exactly what it was," Jessica admitted. "It was at school. But I can't remember what."

"Do you think the smell would be a way to track the thing?" Jason asked.

"Well, we didn't smell anything over at the porch where it saw us. And there was no smell across the grass. It was only where the snake disappeared into the bushes. It may have nothing to do with the creature."

"Maybe the snake made the smell when the hawks came," Jason suggested.

"What do you mean?"

"Well, last year my class went to the center of nature on a field trip."

"You mean the nature center," Jessica interrupted. "Go on."

"Well, they told us that some animals make really bad smells when they are scared or when they want to scare something away. Like a skunk."

"You could be right. That thing didn't seem scared when it saw us at the window. In fact, it seemed angry. But it probably was afraid of those hawks showing up. Way to go squirt, I think you figured out the smell."

The children stood on the lawn for a few more minutes while the stench disappeared. They walked back over to the fern and started carefully lifting the soft branches of the plant to look at the ground. Fortunately, the ground had been recently raked on a yard cleanup day, and they found bare dirt under the fern.

"Look," Jason said as he pointed to tracks on the ground. "Bird prints."

"You're right," Jessica confirmed. "And I think that squiggly mark there is the snake trail."

"Cool, we can track it then."

"I was thinking about something."

"What is that?" Jason asked.

"Well the thing wasn't scared of us. And it had some pretty nasty looking teeth."

"They looked really sharp."

"Maybe we should take something for protection," Jessica suggested and then quickly added, "Just in case. But I don't think there'll be a problem."

Jason reached into his pocket "I've got Dad's old knife," Jason said, as he opened his hand revealing the small pocket knife.

Jessica held her tongue; she didn't feel like seeing a reminder of their Dad at the moment. Silently she turned and went to the garden shed. Jason could hear her rummaging among the gardening tools. In a few minutes his sister emerged from the shed with an old broken axe handle and a broom handle. She handed the axe handle to her brother and kept the broom handle for herself.

"They make good walking sticks," she said. "And we can use them to protect ourselves, as a last resort."

"Good idea," Jason agreed as he brushed some spider webs from the handle.

With Jessica leading the way, the pair began tracking the snake and bird tracks through the bushes. Losing the trail twice, because of heavy leaf cover on the ground and a patch of gravel, the siblings soon found themselves on the path that led from their yard to the old dirt road. The tracks led up the road towards the pond where Jason had seen the witch the day before. The children had followed the tracks for about twenty feet when they stopped and looked closely at the ground.

"The snake tracks stop here," Jessica pointed out.

"And look, the bird tracks stop almost at the same place."

"It doesn't look like there was a fight here," Jessica observed. "The tracks just end. But look here."

Jessica knelt at a spot two feet away, "There are new tracks here. They are kind of round. It looks like two round little feet, kind of like a…"

"Goat," Jason finished her sentence. "Just like at Uncle Chet's farm."

"You mean Great Uncle Chet," Jessica corrected her brother. "You're right; the tracks look kind of like goat hooves. A little smaller and rounder, but very similar."

"You think it turned back into the red thing?" Jason asked.

"I think so," Jessica muttered. "I wonder why the bird tracks stopped."

"Maybe the bird flew off," Jason suggested.

"Or decided to follow the creature from the air," Jessica surmised. "Let's follow the new tracks then."

"Good idea."

The children continued following the tracks up the old dirt road towards Wexler's Pond and the Redwood Glen. The tracks wound their way up the dirt road. Most of the tracks went along the right side of the road but at times the tracks would stray to the opposite side of the road. As Jessica and Jason came to a bend in the road, they noticed a jumble of the small hoof marks. It appeared as if the creature had run around in circles so that there were no clear tracks. Jason squatted and poked his fingers into the dust. He withdrew his fingers and his sister noticed he had withdrawn a feather from the dirt. Blowing off the dust, he then held it up in the sunlight to get a good look at the feather.

"It looks like it could belong to a hawk," Jessica said softly.

"You think the hawk might have caught up with the thing here?"

"Probably," Jessica said looking around. "I don't see any more feathers, but I also don't see any more tracks."

"Maybe the hawk got the thing and flew off with it like yesterday with the snake."

"You could be right," she said. "Can I see the feather?"

Jason handed the feather to his sister and was puzzled as she brought it close to her nose and sniffed.

"What are you doing?" he asked.

"Smell this," she replied, extending the feather to her brother.

Hesitantly Jason leaned forward and took a sniff at the feather. He wrinkled his nose and complained, "Ew, that smells awful."

"Don't you think it smells like what we smelled back in our yard?"

"Yes, that's the smell. It is almost gone now," he added. taking another whiff.

"I thought so," Jessica confirmed. "I just remembered what I smelled at school that reminds me of this smell."

"What was it?" Jason asked as he took the feather back and smoothed it with his fingers.

"A boy in my class did a science experiment to demonstrate how a volcano works. He burned something in it that gives a smell like a volcano might give off."

"What did he burn?"

"It was a powder called sulfur. And the smell was a lot like this smell."

Jason sniffed the feather once more and could no longer smell the nasty odor. He took the feather and stuck the hard tip into a small crack at the top of his walking stick giving it a creative flair.

"What do we do now since the trail is gone?" Jason asked his big sister. Jessica was about to respond when the still summer air was shattered by an unearthly scream.

7

The Witch of Redwood Glen

J ason instinctively moved close to his sister and raised his walking stick as if it were a club. Jessica placed her hand reassuringly on her brother's shoulder and listened carefully as the scream faded.

Leaning close to her brother she whispered, "That came from Wexler's Pond. If we go through the trees to our left, we can sneak up to the pond without anyone seeing us."

Jason nodded in agreement and followed closely behind his sister as she made a trail through the trees and brush by the side of the road. Jessica moved quietly through the woods and paused once to point to a small bush and pretend to scratch her arm. Jason understood this to mean that the plant was poison oak, and he needed to avoid it. He was grateful that his sister had more camping experience than he did because he would have likely walked right through the plant without thinking.

A few minutes of winding back and forth through the trees led the duo to the edge of the clearing. Kneeling down next to a young redwood tree, Jessica peered through the branches of a large bush. Her brother lay down on the reddish dirt and looked under the bush to the clearing.

"Over on the big log," Jessica whispered to her brother.

Shifting his gaze from the far side of Wexler's Pond, he looked to where there was an eight-foot section of a fallen log. There was a circle of rocks that was often used for small camp fires by the few people who knew of the pond's location. Slumped over on the log was a wild-haired woman. Her hair was light grey and so unkempt that it seemed to shoot out in all directions. Her body seemed to be trembling, and when she sat upright the children could see the woman was cradling something in her arms.

"It's the witch," Jason hissed softly.

"She's the person you saw yesterday?"

"Yep, I wonder if she's been casting a spell or something."

"I don't know," Jessica responded. "She seems to have something in her arms."

The children looked intently as the woman lowered the object to her lap and then lifted it gently with her hands to examine it. The children gasped in dismay as they realized the object was a small furry animal. It hung limply in her hands and appeared completely lifeless.

"Is it dead?" Jason asked with concern.

"It looks that way," Jessica whispered back. "I think she's crying, but I can't be sure."

The children watched for several more minutes, and finally Jessica whispered to her brother, "I'm going to try and get a better look. You stay here and I'm going to work around behind where she is sitting."

"No way," Jason hissed back. "I'm going with you."

Jessica shook her head, and in response her brother adamantly nodded his.

"Both of us going might make too much noise," Jessica argued.

"I can be as quiet as you can."

"Can't."

"Can."

The bickering continued until the siblings had become completely oblivious to the old woman on the log. About the third time through their "can-can't" exchange, the old woman had stood and begun walking up the trail on the far side of Wexler's Pond.

Jason looked briefly through the brush and realized the woman was leaving, "She's leaving, let's follow her."

Jessica had to pull her brother to the ground before he could squirm through the bushes and into the clearing.

"You can't just go out there—she'll see you. We've got to circle around the clearing and follow her by going through the woods."

Jason nodded in agreement and eagerly followed his sister as she began weaving her way through the brush and trees. Jessica wasn't quite as careful in not disturbing the bushes and leaves as she circled the pond area. She reasoned that the woman was far enough down the trail that she wouldn't hear a few twigs snap or leaves crunch. She did, however, walk a bit hunched over to conceal herself behind the brush.

As the children got to the point in the brush that was nearest to the log Jessica suddenly stopped and turned to her brother. Tapping the side of her nose she muttered, "Smell it?"

Jason paused and sniffed the air. The odor was faint, but he caught a hint of the horrible smell they now associated with the red snake. "It was here," he whispered as they continued around the pond. By the time they reached the head of the trail, they could see the old woman disappearing around a hillside about a quarter of a mile down the trail.

"I think we should risk going down the trail. Otherwise she's going to get so far ahead we'll lose her," Jessica suggested as she pushed her way through a large fern and stepped onto the trail. Jason followed closely behind, and the duo jogged quietly up the trail, following in the footsteps of the old woman. As they neared the hillside, the trail curved around. They slowed their pace and walked close to the edge of the trail. Cautiously, they crept up to the bend in the trail. Glancing around the corner, they saw that the trail extended about one hundred feet before it turned again. The old woman was not in sight. Using the footprints in the dirt as their guide, the children hurried further along the trail.

"Hold up," Jessica commanded her brother. "We have to be careful as we approach the next bend."

"Ok," Jason agreed, and the children crept carefully up to the bend in the trail. Once again there was no sign of the old woman. The trail curved slightly for fifty feet and came to an end.

"She vanished," Jason muttered. "I told you she's a witch."

Jessica ignored her brother's comment and walked slowly along the trail. She watched the ground closely and noticed the footprints veered off the trail and into the bushes. Jason was not as careful as his sister and began pushing forward into the bushes where the tracks of the woman led.

Suddenly a shrill voice screamed, "You killed him!" Spinning around, the children were confronted by the old woman. She had circled around behind them and stood blocking the trail and their only means of escape.

Grabbing her brother by the arm, she told him in low tones, "She's too old to catch us, run for it."

The children ran back down the trail at the woman. Attempting to escape her grasp, they ran close to the edge of the trail. Branches grabbed at their legs and arms, but fear of capture overwhelmed the slight pain of the branches stinging their bare skin. Jessica sensed the woman reaching out for her, and she instinctively pulled away. Her movement put her close enough to a scraggly, dead tree that a branch raked across her head and pulled at her long hair. Clearing the grasp of the woman she lengthened her stride and continued her race back down the trail.

"Keep going Jason," she called back to encourage her brother. "Give it all you got! We'll be okay once we reach the pond."

Jessica's lungs began to ache a bit as she reached the clearing surrounding Wexler's Pond. Stopping at the water's edge, she bent over and placed her hands on her knees to catch her breath. Remembering what her P.E. teacher had taught her class she then stood up straight to take in more air and raised her hands behind her head.

"Mrs. Deol taught us in P.E. that if you raise your hands after a hard run you can breathe easier," she said as she turned to talk to her brother.

"Jason?" she spun around, looking back up the trail and exclaimed, "Oh no! The witch has Jason!"

8

Mrs. Murphy's Mustache

Jason had tried to dodge around the old woman. Unfortunately, his left foot disagreed with his right on how best to accomplish that task. His fumbling feet sent him sprawling headlong into a wild boysenberry bush that grew on the edge of the trail. His first thought was that the witch had cast a spell on him which kept him from getting up and running away. The more he struggled to get to his feet, the more hopelessly tangled he became in the thorny vines of the plant. Looking hopefully down the trail, his heart sank when he realized Jessica was nowhere in sight. He felt the hand of the witch grasp his upper arm, and he knew he had been caught by the witch of Redwood Glen.

The grip on his arm never loosened as the old woman worked Jason out of the boysenberry vines. Wincing as the sharp stickers of the plant poked and scraped his skin, he fought back tears and did his best to be brave. Once he was free of the vines, the old woman helped the boy to his feet and surveyed her prisoner. Jason dropped his gaze to the ground, fearful of facing the witch.

"Let's get a look at you boy," the woman commanded. Jason stood perfectly still and kept his eyes focused on the ground. He could feel her gaze falling heavily on him.

"Look at me," she added firmly. Jason resisted obeying the old woman and kept his eyes averted. Realizing the child wasn't going to obey her, the woman placed her hand under Jason's chin and lifted his face to meet her gaze.

"Well you aren't one of them at least," the old woman said. "Did you have anything to do with this?"

The old woman released his chin and withdrew something from her coat pocket. When she opened her hand Jason saw a small grey squirrel lying lifeless on her palm.

"It's just a baby," Jason said softly, tears welling in his eyes. "What happened to it?"

"Somebody killed it. Somebody or something."

"Something? You mean like another animal?" Jason asked.

"Something worse," the old woman said ominously. "You've got some pretty good scratches on you. Come along with me and we'll get you cleaned up. Then you can tell me what you are doing on my property."

Realizing he had little choice in the matter, Jason went along with the old woman to the end of the trail. The brush and trees grew thick there, and no trail was in evidence. Looking up at the woman expectantly, he waited for her to cast a spell or say a magic word so that a pathway would open. Gazing down at the young boy, the woman flashed him a crooked smile and simply said, "Follow me to the two giants."

"First red creatures, red snakes, and a witch," thought Jason as he felt an involuntary shudder work through his body, "now giants."

Then taking the boy by his hand, she walked towards two redwood trees that grew very close together. Turning sideways, she eased herself between the trees and urged Jason to follow.

Looking up at the towering redwoods he followed her lead and stepped between the trees.

"Two giants," he said as he smiled up at the trees. He could imagine faces peering down at him from the tops of the twin trees. On the other side of the trees was an opening in the brush about the size of his closet back home. With Jason following closely behind her, the woman walked a few feet to her right and then down a small path that wound its way through a maze of trees and large ferns. A few zigs and a couple of zags through the greenery, and the odd looking pair stepped into a small clearing.

"Cool," Jason whistled as he saw a small log cabin nestled among a sea of wild flowers. The flowers were everywhere including the roof of the cabin. Every inch of the roof appeared to be alive with color. "That is some awesome magic trick."

"Magic?" the old woman replied. Chuckling, she added, "I guess it is a kind of magic how an ugly little seed could turn into something so beautiful. But it's no trick. Just nature doing what nature does best, painting beautiful pictures."

"So it's not magic?"

"You sound disappointed," the old woman said as she took Jason by the hand and led him down a cobblestone pathway to the front of the log cabin.

"I just thought that since you are a…" he paused as he realized what he was going to say might anger the woman.

"You thought it was done by magic because some people think I must be a witch?"

Looking up at the woman, Jason's eyes widened, and he nodded slowly. Rather than being angry, she smiled sweetly in much the same way his grandmother did whenever he would draw a picture or pick her some flowers.

"No son, I'm not a witch. I just live a bit differently than most folks, and some people can't understand different."

The woman led Jason onto the small porch at the front of the cabin. Large bundles of flowers hung upside down from the ceiling of the porch. A single, well-worn rocking chair sat at one end of the porch with a covered wicker basket next to it on the floor. Opening the front door, the woman ushered Jason inside and pointed to an old wooden chair. Following the unspoken direction, the boy settled onto the chair and began examining his surroundings as his hostess busied herself rooting through a cabinet in the small kitchen.

While the small cabin seemed to have some object of interest in every nook and cranny, everywhere he looked was tidy and clean. Some of the items he had seen before—but, only in antique stores when his Grandpa Phil would drag him along on buying trips. Many other objects looked very old and unusual.

"Here we go," the woman said as she set a brown bottle and small box on the table next to Jason. Taking a cotton ball from the box, she opened the bottle and placed the ball on the mouth of the bottle. Tilting the bottle slightly she dampened the cotton ball and began dabbing the scratches on Jason's knees with the moistened ball. He winced as the cotton ball made his scratches sting once again.

"I should have warned you it might sting a bit," the woman said.

"It's okay. My mom uses the purple stuff, and it stings too."

"So tell me what you were doing so far into the woods with your friend."

"That wasn't my..." Jason paused as he thought about what he should reveal to the old woman.

"Let me guess," the woman interjected. "She wasn't your friend, so that probably means she is your sister or other relative. Am I right?"

"Yes, she's my sister."

"What is your name son?"

Jason remained quiet for a moment.

"Let me try that again," the old woman said, extending her hand. "My name is Mrs. Murphy. And you would be?"

Recalling his manners Jason placed his hand in the woman's and shook it. "Nice to meet you Mrs. Murphy. My name is Jason Cowell."

"Very nice to meet you Jason Cowell. Cowell, I don't know of any Cowells in the area."

"We just moved here. My Mom grew up around here and we just moved back after..."

Jason jumped slightly as a scratching noise interrupted his response. His eyes widened as he looked around for the source of the noise.

"Don't worry," Mrs. Murphy said reassuringly. "That will be my cat wanting in."

She strode over to the cabin door and opened it. "Come on in my friend."

A lean orange cat entered the room and rubbed softly against Mrs. Murphy's legs as he passed her. The cat looked around the room and spied Jason. Cautiously walking towards the seated boy, the cat flared its nose slightly to take in its surrounding more completely.

"Jason Cowell meet Moustache, Moustache meet Jason Cowell."

Jason giggled at the name of the cat. "Moustache? That's a silly name. Why moustache?"

As if in response to the question, Moustache leapt onto Jason's lap and began sniffing his face.

"Oh, I see," Jason laughed. "He has a white moustache."

Jason was concentrating on the cat so much that he had failed to notice that Mrs. Murphy had grabbed a straw house broom and was holding it like a baseball bat. She tensed her muscles and began to swing the broom towards Jason.

9

The Fallen

"Look out Jason!" Jessica screamed as she burst through the front door of Mrs. Murphy's cabin.

The warning came too late as the broom came crashing down striking its target firmly on the head. Jason fell backward in the chair toppling over in the entryway to the kitchen. Moustache didn't fare as well as the blow struck him soundly on the top of his head. A rapid second blow sent his furry orange body hurtling towards the front door of the cabin.

Jessica ran at Mrs. Murphy to stop her from using the broom on her brother, "You better not hit my brother again!"

Grasping the broom in Mrs. Murphy's hands she attempted to wrestle it from the old woman. The old lady was remarkably strong and was able to wrench the broom away from Jessica and then moved with speed towards the front door. By the time she reached the door Moustache was scurrying across the porch.

"Are you a crazy woman?" Jessica cried out.

"No Jess, she's okay," Jason said in Mrs. Murphy's defense.

"But she hit you with the broom."

"No, she hit Moustache."

"Moustache?" came the bewildered reply.

"Her cat. Only I have the feeling it wasn't really her cat."

"You are right Jason," Mrs. Murphy said as she reentered her cabin. Her face was white and she looked worried. "It smells pretty bad out there right now so don't go outside for a few minutes."

The children caught a hint of the stench they now associated with the red creatures they were tracking. Jason wrinkled his nose and finally couldn't help but pinch off his nostrils. Jessica exhaled through her nose to get the offending odor from settling into her nostrils.

"It was one of them Jess," Jason said softly. "Only it was a cat this time."

"This time?" Mrs. Murphy repeated. "You've seen them before?"

"Yes," Jason said. "We've seen them a couple of times now. In fact we were…"

"Shush Jason," Jessica interrupted.

"It's okay, Mrs. Murphy is a nice lady. She wasn't trying to hurt me."

"I wasn't going to hurt Jason," Mrs. Murphy said reassuringly. "I didn't want that thing to hurt your brother. Who knows what it might have done."

"But how did you know it wasn't your cat?" Jessica asked.

Before Mrs. Murphy could answer Jason spoke up, "It was the eyes wasn't it?"

"That's right Jason. When I saw his eyes I knew it wasn't my Moustache."

"I didn't spot them until we were nose to nose," Jason confessed. "I'm sure glad you spotted them Mrs. Murphy."

"Me too Jason," the woman said as helped the boy back into the chair. Turning to Jessica she added, "We haven't been properly introduced. I'm Mrs. Murphy and you must be Jason's sister."

"I'm Jessica," she confirmed. "Thank you for helping my brother."

"Think nothing of it," Mrs. Murphy said with a smile. "I don't think we started off on the right foot back at the trail. I must have given you quite a scare."

"Yes it did. Jason we had better be going and let the, and let Mrs. Murphy get back to what she was doing."

Mrs. Murphy chuckled a little at Jessica's slip of the tongue, "Jason do you still believe I am a witch?"

Looking up at Mrs. Murphy's face the boy smiled softly and shook his head, "No ma'am. You are just a nice lady who loves nature."

Mrs. Murphy smiled at the boy's response and turned to Jessica. "I may be a bit different Jessica, but I am not a witch. I just wanted to know who was on my property."

"And she wanted to know who killed the baby squirrel," Jason added. "Isn't that right Mrs. Murphy?"

"That's right Jason. Let's finish cleaning you up. Jessica if you wouldn't mind going in the kitchen there is some cold lemonade in the refrigerator. You will find glasses in the cupboard to the left of the sink."

Jessica hesitated for a moment. "It will give you a chance to make sure I don't have any spider legs, eyes of newts or lizard tails around," Mrs. Murphy chuckled. The humor of the hostess helped Jessica feel more at ease and she followed Mrs. Murphy's directions and set about filling three glasses with lemonade.

"So when did you first see the Fallen?" Mrs. Murphy asked Jason as she dabbed hydrogen peroxide on the scratches covering his arms and face.

"The Fallen?" Jessica inquired.

"Those nasty shape shifters like the one that was pretending to be my Moustache."

"So that's what they are called," Jason said.

"Well that is what I have always called them since I was a little Willie."

"A little what?" Jason asked.

Mrs. Murphy laughed loudly. "I guess that does sound funny. Let me ask you this, have you ever had something happen that you had wished really hard about? Something that isn't normal?"

Jason's jaw dropped and his eyes got as big as saucers. He began nodding and fixed his gaze on Mrs. Murphy's eyes. Smiling at the boy she dabbed at a scratch on his nose.

"Well we always felt that we had willed things to happen. So we called ourselves Willies. It was about the time we started calling ourselves the Willies that we began seeing the Fallen."

"What are the Fallen?" Jessica asked. "You called them shifters or something."

"Shape shifters dear. There are folk stories from around the world that talk about animals or people that can change shapes.

In my time I have seen the Fallen change into or out of many different forms."

"Why are they called the Fallen? Why not shifters or something like that?" Jason interjected.

"Well there is a story behind that. I will make you a deal, you tell me your Willie story and I will tell you the story of where the Fallen get their name."

Jason looked to his sister before saying anything. Jessica nodded her approval and Jason responded by extending his hand, "You've got a deal."

Mrs. Murphy cleaned up her first aid supplies and absentmindedly stuck her hands in her coat pockets, "Oh dear, I seemed to have forgotten something. Let me just take care of the little one and we can get to the stories. Oh where has the time gone? It's lunch time and I bet with all you two have done this morning you must be hungry."

Until she had mentioned lunch the siblings hadn't realized that the morning was gone and they indeed were feeling hunger pangs.

"Maybe we should come back another time then," Jessica suggested.

"It has been so long since I have had guests in my home I would love it if you would stay and have lunch with me."

"We've been enough of a bother to you already Mrs. Murphy," the young girl said.

"Oh it's no bother my dear. In fact it would be a joy."

"Can we Jess?" Jason pleaded.

"Only if we can help," Jessica responded. "We've got some snacks in my backpack."

"Good, we will make it a potluck then. I can make some sandwiches and we can have more lemonade."

"I will take care of the baby squirrel for you Mrs. Murphy," Jason volunteered.

"Baby squirrel?" Jessica asked.

"It was what she was holding down by the pond," Jason explained. "Someone killed it. Or something. Right Mrs. Murphy?"

"Yes child, or something."

"You mean the Fallen?" Jessica asked anxious to know their story.

"Yes my dear. I do think it was one of the Fallen."

Mrs. Murphy gave Jason the small squirrel and directed him to the far side of the vegetable garden where she had a small plot of ground which she used as an animal graveyard. Once their hands were washed Jessica and Mrs. Murphy set about in the kitchen fixing tuna sandwiches. Soon the trio was gathered back at the table eating lunch as Jason told the story of his Willie experience.

10

Mrs. Murphy's Story

"T"hank you for lunch Mrs. Murphy," Jessica said politely as she helped clean the table.

"Yes, thank you Mrs. Murphy. You make tuna just like my Mom does," Jason added.

"Well thank you for the compliment Jason, but it was your sister who made the tuna so delicious. Thank you two for bringing the Cheetos and Double Stuft Oreo cookies. They really made the lunch complete."

As the trio finished cleaning up after the meal Jason's impatience had worn as thin as it could get.

"Can you tell us the story now Mrs. Murphy? The story of the Fallen?" he said anxiously.

Chuckling softly the old woman replied, "Yes dear, I can tell you the story now. But why don't we move outside? It is such a beautiful day and we can enjoy the flowers and the giants while I tell the story."

"The giants?" Jessica asked suspiciously.

"The trees," her brother replied.

"The redwoods my dear. I like to think of them as giants who guard this place."

Moving outside Mrs. Murphy guided the children to a bench in the middle of the flowers. The bench was a ten foot section of a redwood tree that had been cut down decades before. A wedge cut from the log formed a seat and back to the bench. Years of use had worn the wood to a shiny smooth surface and proved to be quite comfortable.

"This is my favorite listening spot in the garden," Mrs. Murphy said as they trio settled onto the bench.

"Listening spot?" Jessica inquired.

"I like to sit and listen to the sounds all around me. I listen to the animals, the wind, and trees. And sometimes I hear other sounds."

"Other sounds?" Jason piped up.

"Let's just see what you might hear," Mrs. Murphy said mysteriously. "You never know what you might hear. As for right now I believe you want to hear a story."

"Yes," Jason said eagerly. Though trying to appear reserved Jessica's eyes revealed that she too was anxious to hear the story of the Fallen.

"Well this is a story about an amazing kingdom and a very kind and loving king," Mrs. Murphy began.

"Shouldn't the story begin once upon a time?" Jason interrupted.

"If it were a fairy tale perhaps," responded the old lady. "Or a story of some long ago time and places that no longer exists. You see I believe this story is true and not a fairy tale. It is also a story that took place long ago. Yet it takes place now and will continue on for a long time to come. So to say once upon a time would limit the story. And by doing so it would limit the goodness of the king and the greatness of his kingdom."

"The people in the kingdom were shape shifters right?" Jessica asked thoughtfully.

"You are a smart one aren't you?" Mrs. Murphy said with a smile. "Pretty and smart. Yes, the inhabitants of the kingdom were and are shape shifters. If it helps to refer to them as people we can call them that. Yet they have powers we can only imagine. The king has a reputation for being a very benevolent king. That means he cares for all of those in his kingdom and he wants the very best for his people. It also means that the decisions he makes and the things he does benefit his people. Though sometimes the people in his kingdom don't understand everything he does or why he does them."

"It sounds like a wonderful place," Jason said, his eyes growing bigger with each bit of the story.

"It certainly does," Mrs. Murphy agreed. "And it would be wonderful to live in a kingdom where the king cares about all of his subjects. The kingdom is a wonderful place but not every one of the king's people are happy. The king's assistant became jealous of the king and the king's power. He began thinking he could be an even better ruler than the king was. And somehow he convinced many of the king's subjects that he would make a better king.

"But where the king was kind and benevolent, the assistant was cruel and selfish. Unlike the king he didn't care about the good of all the people, he wanted the power and glory that being king could bring him. The assistant decided that he would try to take the throne by force and he led a revolt against the king."

"Are the Fallen the assistant's followers?" Jason asked, his eyes dancing with excitement at the story. "And who is the assistant?"

"Well I don't know what his name really is but I have always called the assistant the Pretender," Mrs. Murphy replied. "And yes, the Fallen are what I have called the followers of the Pretender."

"What happened with the revolt?" Jessica asked eagerly.

"Well the Pretender and his followers were relentless, but the forces of the king were stronger. Despite the many followers the Pretender had swayed away from the king, there were twice as many followers of the king than there were Fallen. Still the Pretender and his followers did a great deal of damage in their attempt to take over."

"So the good king won in the end?" Jason asked.

"Well yes and no. His people won the battle for the kingdom, but the fight continues to this day. The Pretender and his followers have spread out throughout the world and seek to destroy any lives they can. The King has sent out his followers as Guardians to protect as many people as they can."

"So the Fallen that changed into Moustache was trying to attack Jason?" Jessica asked with a great deal of concern in her tone.

"Perhaps," Mrs. Murphy replied. "He may have wanted to attack Jason, or attack me. On the other hand he might have been snooping around for information or looking for something I might have in my house. You never know with the Fallen.

They are sneaky and underhanded. You can always count on one thing with the Fallen."

"What is that?" Jason piped up.

"You can count on the fact that they are up to no good. I don't believe you could find even an ounce of goodness in the whole lot of them put together."

"Since the Fallen are so sneaky how can you tell one of them from one of the king's Guardians?" Jessica asked thoughtfully as she pondered Mrs. Murphy's story. "Wouldn't they probably look alike? And if they can change their appearance there is no telling what they might look like."

"Very true my dear," Mrs. Murphy agreed. "The Fallen are quite crafty and can appear very similar to one of the Guardians. Or as you saw today they can appear in the form of my beloved Moustache. Over the years I have encountered many Fallen, but I have also met my share of Guardians. And there is one thing that the Fallen can never get right when they change their appearance."

"The eyes," Jason said softly as if he might be giving away a secret to a member of the Fallen trying to eavesdrop on the conversation.

"That's right Jason. The Fallen never seem to get the eyes right. They seem hollow as if there is nothing behind them. There is a saying that the eyes are the window to the soul. If that is true it must mean the Fallen have no souls."

"What about the Guardians?" Jessica asked. "What are their eyes like?"

"They are beautiful eyes, so full of life and light. They fairly sparkle and shine and make you feel safe and secure. Just as you could never forget the cold darkness of the Fallen's eyes, I think you will find that you also can't forget the wonderful brilliance of a Guardian's eyes."

"It is hard to imagine one of those ugly little red creatures having beautiful eyes," Jessica murmured.

"Well I have never seen one of the Guardians appear in that form before. I don't know what they look like naturally. But I imagine they must be as beautiful as their eyes appear," Mrs. Murphy said wistfully and then suddenly put her finger to her lips indicating for the children to be quiet. Smiling she put her hand to her ear and listened thoughtfully.

The children strained to hear what the old woman was listening to. Suddenly Jason began looking all around for the source of what he now heard.

"Who is it?" Jason whispered.

"What are you talking about?" Jessica asked.

"The voices," her brother responded softly causing the young girl to listen more intently.

11

Voices, Giants and a Stealthy Prowler

L ifting her head high Jessica closed her eyes and listened for the voices her brother had heard. At first she heard nothing but the wind in the trees. Then slowly a smile appeared on her face.

"I hear it now," Jessica sighed happily. "It isn't voices, is it Mrs. Murphy?"

"No dear. But I have the feeling you know what it is."

"Yes," the girl responded. "I think I do. It could sound a bit like voices, but I know that sound very well. I am just used to hearing it much louder."

"What is it?" Jason prodded.

"It's the ocean."

"That's right my dear. When the wind is blowing just right it carries the sound of waves breaking on the shore and I can hear them here. In fact the best place to hear them is right where we are sitting. That is why I call it my listening spot. What else can you hear?"

The children sat concentrating on the sounds around them and softly began listing off what they heard.

"Wind in the trees," Jessica started.

"A squirrel chewing on something over by that rock," Jason added.

"I hear birds in the trees."

"What kind of birds?" Mrs. Murphy prodded.

"I'm not sure," Jessica admitted.

"I hear a mocking bird," Jason piped up.

"That's right. There is also a crow in the distance."

"I hear something walking in dried leaves," Jessica said suddenly and turned to look for the source of the sound. Finally she spied the culprit. An orange tail was weaving its way through a maze of zinnias. "I think it is Moustache!"

"Maybe it is one of the Fallen again," Jason cautioned his sister as he followed her gaze and spotted the tail.

"Jason could be right," Mrs. Murphy added. "Although after the thrashing I gave the last one I don't think they would choose to change into Moustache again. I do hope it is my Moustache. I've been afraid they might have hurt him."

All eyes were fixed on the tail as it flicked back and forth through the colorful flowers. Jessica found herself holding her breath as an orange head emerged from beneath the canopy of flowers.

"Is it?" Jason whispered.

"Moustache!" Mrs. Murphy elatedly called as she saw the familiar cat eyes of her beloved companion. "It is you!"

The orange cat bounced over to his old friend and began rubbing against her leg. His purring added another sound to the afternoon air as the children happily stroked his soft fur.

"He doesn't seem to be injured," Jessica reported as she searched for any signs of wounds.

"Moustache was probably off hunting and one of those horrid little Fallen took advantage of his absence knowing I would let him in my home," Mrs. Murphy surmised. "I am so glad you are alright my old friend. You missed a wonderful lunch but it will soon be time for your dinner."

"I've lost track of the time," Jessica said suddenly at Mrs. Murphy's mention of dinner. "Does anybody know what time it is?"

"I have a clock inside the house," Mrs. Murphy offered.

"One second," Jason said and began digging into his pockets. His fingers begin searching through the many objects he brought along on their journey. Locating a flat glass and metal disk he withdrew a wristwatch that had been missing its band for many years. "It is, um, let's see. It is two…"

Looking over at the watch in her brother's hand Jessica stated, "It is three fifteen. We should be heading home."

"Oh do you have to?" the tone of disappointment was clear in the woman's voice. "I have really enjoyed having the two of you visit me. I'm just sorry the whole day started off on the wrong foot."

"I'm sorry we were spying on you," Jessica said humbly. "And I am sorry we were on your property without permission."

"Yes ma'am, I'm sorry too," Jason added. "And I'm really sorry I thought you were a witch."

Mrs. Murphy chuckled enthusiastically and then turned to Jessica, "Have you made up your mind about me Jessica?"

Blushing Jessica looked up into the woman's kind face and spontaneously embraced her hostess. Hugging her close around her neck the young girl softly said, "I think you are a wonderful lady and I am so lucky I got to meet you. There is no way you could ever be a witch."

As Jessica slowly released her grip on the woman she couldn't help but note tears had welled up in the old woman's sparkling eyes.

"That means the world to me my dear," Mrs. Murphy said with a smile. "I do hope the two of you will come back and visit me often. You are welcome here any time."

"Can we come back soon Jess?" Jason pleaded.

"As long as we aren't a bother to Mrs. Murphy," Jessica insisted.

"The two of you a bother? Never!"

"We really have to get home," Jessica reiterated. "But we will be back soon."

"The sooner the better," Mrs. Murphy responded. "Don't forget to get your knapsack my dear. I want to walk the two of you home so I know you get back safely."

"We can find our way with no problem," Jessica insisted. "We have taken so much of your time already."

"Taken my time? You gave me time Jessica. Spending the afternoon with the two of you has given me a wonderful day that I might never have experienced. After all it isn't every day that I get to smack one of the Fallen on the head," Mrs. Murphy added with a chuckle.

"It's an awful long walk Mrs. Murphy," Jason said in agreement with his sister.

"I will tell you what," the lady bargained. "I will walk back with you to the edge of my property. That will let me know you are on the right path and give me a little needed exercise."

The children agreed to this arrangement and Jessica retrieved her backpack from the log cabin. As they followed the cobblestone path back the way they had entered the redwood glen Mrs. Murphy would point out various flowers and plants and ask the children if they knew the name. Some the children knew readily and others the woman would tell them the popular name of the plant or flower. Two large rocks marked the entrance to the winding narrow pathway that would lead them back to the dirt road. The route out of the glen was easier to spot than the trail into the area where the log cabin sat. Reaching the twin redwoods Jason paused.

"You've met the two giants haven't you?" he asked his sister.

"Giants?" Jessica responded with a note of alarm.

Patting one of the redwoods he added, "These giants guard the entrance to Mrs. Murphy's magical garden."

Smiling the young girl patted the two giants and slipped between them to the gravel path on the other side. Jason and Mrs. Murphy followed close behind. Once they were on the gravel road the siblings knew which way to head. The trio chatted cheerfully as they walked among the towering redwoods and soon arrived at the clearing where Wexler's Pond sat sparkling in the sun.

12

Watching Eyes

"We are almost to edge of my property," Mrs. Murphy said as she and the children began walking around the edge of Wexler's Pond.

"Wexler's Pond is yours?" Jason asked in amazement.

"Yes it is. My grandfather found it and gave it the family name."

"But I thought your name was Murphy," the boy said a bit bewildered.

"Wexler is my maiden name Jason. My grandfather James Wexler owned this land and then it became my father's land. My father was John Wexler. And now the property is mine. I married a man with the last name of Murphy so that is my name now. But I am still a Wexler."

"Maiden name?" Jason asked still a bit perplexed.

"That means unmarried name, right Mrs. Murphy?"

"That's right Jessica. Just like Cowell is Jessica's maiden name. Someday when she is married she will probably have a different last name."

"Just like Mom," Jessica explained. "Her maiden name is Thomas. Just like her parent's last names. When she got married she went from Wendy Thomas to Wendy Cowell."

"I get it now," Jason said. "I think."

"Well when you get married someday your wife will become a Cowell," Jessica added.

"Ew gross!" Jason exclaimed. "I'm not getting married. Especially not to any old girl."

Mrs. Murphy chuckled, "Things change Jason. Someday you might change your mind."

"Never!" Jason said adamantly.

"We'll see," Jessica said taunting her little brother.

"You said your mother was Wendy Thomas?" Mrs. Murphy asked.

"Yes, that was her maiden name," Jessica confirmed.

"And she used to live around here when she was growing up?"

"Yes, she said she grew up on Redwood Court."

"Do people say you look like her Jessica?" Mrs. Murphy asked.

"They say that all the time," Jason chimed in.

"Then I believe I knew your mother when she lived here."

"Really?" Jessica asked. "You know our mother?"

"Well I knew her a long time ago," Mrs. Murphy said with a smile. "What a wonderful young lady she was, and I imagine she still is to have two great children like you. And I think if you look deep enough you will find you have much more in common with your mother than just her good looks."

"What do you mean?" the girl asked.

"That is a puzzle to solve another day," the old woman said with a twinkle in her eyes. "Be sure to tell your mother hello from me. And be sure to bring her up to see me some time. I would love to see the woman she has grown up to be."

"Okay," Jason said eagerly.

"You two had better run along now. Your mother is probably worried about where you have been all day."

The siblings turned and started heading down the road when Jason suddenly stopped and ran back to give Mrs. Murphy a hug around her waist. Her smile broadened and she bent down to give the boy a hug in return. No sooner had she hugged Jason than she felt Jessica's arms wrap around her shoulders as well.

"Thank you for everything," Jessica said enthusiastically.

"Yes," Jason agreed. "And thank you for not being a witch."

"Thank you two for brightening my day."

Mrs. Murphy smiled as she watched her two new friends disappear down the old dirt road. Once the children were out of her sight she turned and walked casually back to her magical garden. She had no idea that several sets of eyes were watching her from the woods. Those eyes were very dark, cold and empty. One set of eyes belonged to a small red creature that reached up with tentacle like fingers to rub a spot on its head. A snarl formed on its thin lips and a low hiss emitted from between the sharp fangs in its mouth.

Jessica and Jason chatted excitedly as they hurried down the dirt road. Their journey had proved more adventurous than they could have imagined. While they had many questions answered by their new friend, each one that had been answered generated several new ones in their inquisitive young minds.

"What are we going to tell mom?" Jason asked.

"I think we can tell her about hiking up the dirt road to Wexler's Pond and meeting Mrs. Murphy. We don't need to mention spying on Mrs. Murphy. And we certainly shouldn't say anything about tracking the Fallen."

"Shouldn't she know about the Fallen? What if they go after her?"

"I've been thinking about that," Jessica said slowly. "If we tell her about the Fallen she might not believe us. Then we can forget about getting permission to explore the dirt road. On the other hand if she believes us she could still keep us from going up the road to protect us from them. I think for now the best thing is to not say anything about them."

"But they still might try and attack her," Jason argued.

"According to Mrs. Murphy the Fallen have been around for a long time. If they had wanted to attack Mom they probably would have already tried don't you think?"

"Well," the boy pondered his sister's theory. "I guess you could be right."

"I'll tell you what," Jessica offered, "if we get any sign that Mom is in danger we will tell her. Even if it means we don't get to go adventuring again. Deal?"

"Deal pickle!" Jason said excitedly as they came to the small path that lead to their yard. "Last one home is a nasty red Fallen!"

Jason broke into a run and began weaving down the pathway. Unable to resist the challenge Jessica charged into the foliage in pursuit of her brother. The narrow pathway made it nearly impossible to pass the boy but she kept close on his heels. As the duo emerged into their backyard Jessica was able to take advantage of her longer legs and sped past her brother and bounded up the steps to the back door.

"Beat ya!" Jessica called over her shoulder.

"Hey! No fair!" Jason argued.

"What do you mean no fair? I beat you to the house fair and square."

Knowing his sister had not cheated during the foot race he dropped his gaze to the back steps. Conceding his sister's victory he admitted in low tones, "I just didn't want to be a nasty red Fallen."

"It's okay," his sister said to comfort him. "You could never be one of those creatures." Then with a giggle she added, "After all not even you smell that bad."

"Hey!" the boy countered. "That's not very nice."

Much like their new friend, the children entered the house completely unaware that multiple sets of eyes were watching their every move. Two sets watched from underneath a large fern in the yard. Those eyes were as dark and vacant as those tracking Mrs. Murphy. Three other sets of eyes looked back and forth between the Fallen under the fern to the children entering the house. These eyes sparkled with life and viewed the scene from a vantage point high up in an ash tree in the neighboring yard. The three red-tailed hawks brought their heads together and if anyone had been close enough to the trio to hear they would have been stunned by the whispered voices coming from the birds.

"Follow the two under the fern but don't let them see you," the apparent leader whispered to the smallest of the birds. "We need to know what they are up to."

The smaller bird nodded and fixed its gaze on the fern in the children's yard where the Fallen were hiding.

"And my assignment Captain?" the third bird inquired.

"Stay with the children," came the hushed response. "I will send reinforcements."

13

A Secret Nearly Revealed

When Wendy Cowell arrived home she found her daughter sitting sideways in the easy chair in the small but tidy family room. Her legs were draped over the arm of the chair and her nose was buried in a mystery novel featuring a heroine Jessica's own age. Jason's body was sprawled across a throw rug in the middle of the floor where he was concentrating on defeating the evil empire that had taken control of the galaxy inside of his favorite Game Boy game.

"Well you two are certainly a sight," their mother declared as she entered the room. "Jessica you know better than to sit on the furniture when you are filthy. You both need a bath. That must have been some hike you went on."

"It was," Jason responded excitedly without taking his eyes off the small screen.

Rolling off the easy chair Jessica stood up and scanned her clothing, "I guess we got dirtier than I thought."

"You certainly did. You can tell me all about your adventures over dinner. But first the two of you need to clean up. Jessica you take the first bath and then come help me with dinner. Jason there are two bags of groceries in the car that need to be brought in and then you can take a bath when your sister is done."

The siblings moaned momentarily but then set about following their mother's instructions. An hour later the children, now bathed and in clean clothes, settled into their seats at the kitchen table. Following a brief blessing of the meal the three

Cowells began serving up teriyaki chicken breast, green beans and applesauce. A short time later as the trio were finishing their meal the conversation turned to the activities of the children.

"So how was your hike today?" Wendy inquired.

"It was great," Jason said enthusiastically.

"Yeah, we had a good time," Jessica agreed. "We actually explored most of the morning and until just before you got home."

"And how many fights did the two of you get into during that time?" their mother quipped.

"None," Jason said in their defense. "We actually didn't fight at all."

"It's true," Jessica confirmed when she saw her mother's eyebrows raise in surprise. "We got along just fine. Probably because we were doing something we both enjoyed."

"So where did you go?"

"We headed up the dirt road to Wexler's Pond," Jessica began. "Then we explored along the path on the other side of the pond."

"You were able to keep your brother out of the pond? That's a first," their mother said referring to Jason's love of swimming wherever he can find water.

"We were too busy," Jason blurted out.

"Too busy?"

"Jason means we were too busy following animal tracks to bother getting wet," Jessica clarified. "We spotted some bird tracks and even a snake track."

"That sounds pretty exciting. I didn't know you the two of you were interested in tracking wildlife. I hope you know the difference between poisonous snakes and safe snakes," Wendy said cautioning her children. "I don't want you to try picking up a snake unless you know it is non-poisonous."

"I don't want to pick up any snakes," Jessica emphatically declared.

"I don't blame you," her mother admitted.

"The only poisonous snakes around here would be rattlesnakes," Jason said confidently. "And they have triangle heads."

"When did you become an expert in snakes Jason?" Wendy asked in amazement.

"I saw snakes at the zoo last month remember? You and Jessica were looking at turtles instead of paying attention to the important stuff," Jason said taking on an air of authority.

"Yes," Wendy said holding back a laugh as Jessica rolled her eyes. "I remember missing the real important stuff. So tell me what I missed."

"Well there was this hugemongous picture of the snakes of California. It showed which snakes were bad and which were good. And around here the only bad ones are rattlesnakes."

"I'll have to pay more attention to, what was that called, hugemongous pictures? You just never know when you might learn something important," his mom said as she acknowledged his expertise on snakes. "So did you find the snake you were tracking?"

"We spotted it," Jessica piped in. "But it was too far away to see very well."

"It wasn't a rattlesnake was it?" Wendy asked with an overtone of concern in her voice.

"Naw," the resident snake expert replied. "Those fat red snakes don't have rattles on 'em. They sure do stink though."

Jason felt a sharp pain in his shin as Jessica kicked him under the table.

"Ow! Mom, Jessica just kicked me!"

"Sorry Jace," Jessica quickly said. "I thought I felt something on my leg and I flinched."

"Watch it will ya!" Jason whined.

"Jason, your sister apologized to you. What do you say?"

"I forgive you," Jason said grudgingly as he rubbed his shin.

"So besides stinky snakes did you see any other animals?"

"We saw some hawks," Jessica responded with enthusiasm.

"Aren't they fascinating birds?" Wendy said.

"They sure are. It's amazing to watch them fly."

"Do we have any books on snakes Mom?" Jason interrupted.

"Jason it is rude to interrupt a conversation," Wendy corrected her son.

"Sorry Mom, but do we have any books on snakes?"

"What am I going to do with you," his mother sighed in exasperation.

"I have a couple of ideas," Jessica snickered.

"No Jason, I don't think we have any books about snakes. But I bet the library has plenty of information about snakes."

"When can we go?" Jason asked enthusiastically.

"Well as it so happens I need to run downtown to run make some copies at the copy shop. We could all go and you and Jessica could explore the library a bit. I think the library is open until eight or nine. Then we could get ice cream cones at the little shop on the corner across from the library."

"Yay!" Jason yelled out. "Ice cream!"

"About those ideas I have on what we can do with Jason…" Jessica started.

"Now Jessica," Wendy said with mock disdain.

"Just kidding Mom," Jessica replied, her eyes sparkling like her mother's. "Just kidding."

Just then Jessica saw some movement over her mother's right shoulder. Her eyes darted in the direction of the movement and she spied the hollow eyes of a Fallen through the window. When the creature realized it had been spotted by Jessica it dropped out of sight below the window sill. Jessica was about to gasp when she caught herself.

"What's the matter Jessica?" her mother asked as she looked up from her plate. "You look like you've seen a ghost."

"Nu, nothing Mom," Jessica stammered as she regained her composure. "I, I just thought I saw someone outside. But it was nothing. Nothing but a branch."

Wendy looked over her shoulder and looked at the window behind her and shrugged her shoulders. "Well if you saw a branch you saw more than I can see. I only see your bicycle lying on the lawn."

"Oh that must have been it," Jessica said half-heartedly.

"Speaking of which," her mother continued. "Where does your bike belong?"

"Sorry Mom," Jessica responded. "I'll move it right after dinner."

Jason was so preoccupied with making designs in the surface of his applesauce that he had missed most of the exchange between his mother and sister. The ring of the telephone brought his awareness back to the conversation at the table. Wendy got up to answer the phone leaving the children alone at the table.

"I saw one of them outside," Jessica said in low tones as she leaned over the table towards Jason.

"A snake?"

"No silly. One of the Fallen!"

"Where?" Jason asked as he looked around anxiously.

"Out there," Jessica pointed to the window where she had seen the face.

Jason scurried over to the window and looked out trying to see the creature. He saw no signs of the Fallen and quickly returned to the table. "What do you think it was doing out there?"

"I think it was doing some spying. Just like the one that pretended to be Moustache." Jessica theorized. "Which means we need to be very careful about who, or what, we let into the house."

"Let what into the house?" Wendy said as she reentered the room.

"Uh, um," Jessica stammered.

"Bugs," Jason said. "And snakes."

"Well good," Wendy agreed. "I don't want to find any bugs or snakes in this house. And that also goes for lizards or other creepy crawlers. Got that little man?"

Jason smiled sheepishly as he remembered the lizard incident in their old house, "Got it Mom."

"Okay you two, let's clean up the table and go downtown."

14

Shhh…It's the Library

With the trio all pitching in, dinner cleanup took a mere fifteen minutes. A short drive into town found Jessica and Jason standing in front of the local branch of the library. The newly repainted Victorian era building gleamed in the warm glow of the early evening sunlight. The sign in the front window showed that the library would be closing at nine that night giving the children more than enough time to explore what the building had to offer.

"Okay kids," Wendy instructed the children. "I will be across the street at the copy shop. So in case you need me you will know where to find me. I will meet you at the ice cream parlor at 8:30 for a treat. Is everybody clear on where to be and when?"

"Yes Mom," Jessica responded brightly.

"Jason?"

"Huh?"

"Were you listening to me?" Wendy asked her son who was obviously preoccupied with a tall tower on the corner of the library building. "Jason?"

"Eight thirty, ice cream. Got it," he said, still fixated on the tower.

"Don't worry Mom," Jessica reassured her mother. "I'll keep track of the munchkin."

"Hey!" Jason said defensively without taking his eyes off the top window of the tower.

"Stay out of trouble you two," Wendy said good naturedly before crossing the street with her book bag full of papers to copy.

Turning to her brother Jessica noticed he was still staring at the tower. "What is so fascinating up there?"

"Just wondering how far you could see from way up there," Jason said absent-mindedly.

"Who knows and who cares. Come on squirt, let's get going," she urged him up the steps.

The building loomed large in front of the siblings. Wide granite steps narrowed as they climbed. Ten, eleven, twelve, thirteen. Thirteen steps to the large wooden doors. Above the ornately carved doors an arched window was painted with the gold numbers 3571. Before entering the library Jason paused and ran his fingers over the front of the Victorian structure.

"Metal," Jason murmured.

"What?" Jessica asked.

"This building feels like metal."

Jessica paused and rapped her knuckles on the front of the building.

"Weird," Jessica responded as she felt the solid metal façade of the library. "It does feel like metal. But we will deal with that another time. We only have so much time you know."

"Time for what?" Jason asked, his mind still dwelling on the metal front of the building and on the tower.

"Time for you to find a book on snakes. And time for me to find out what I can about the Fallen."

"Oh, oh yeah," Jason said as he refocused his attention on snakes.

Jessica asked the librarian at the desk where her brother could find information on snakes. Once she had Jason situated in front of a shelf full of books on snakes and reptiles Jessica set off to find an available computer terminal to search for books on the Fallen.

"Nothing," Jessica sighed after ten minutes of searching the library database. "Wait a minute," she mumbled to herself. "Maybe the name Fallen isn't what I should be searching for. What was that thing Mrs. Murphy called the Fallen?"

Jessica thought for a moment and then typed "shape shifter" into the library's search engine. The screen produced a string of books and periodicals held by the library with information on shape shifters. Jotting down information about several of the more promising entries on scratch paper, Jessica was about to start finding the books on the list when a link on the computer screen caught her eye. Clicking the link the computer brought up the database of archives of the local newspaper. Jessica once again tried entering the keyword Fallen in the search engine. There were no entries where Fallen was a key word in an article. Trying the words shape shifter also yielded no results.

Finally Jessica entered the keywords Murphy and Redwood Glen. Several old articles came up in the list of responses and the young girl's eyes widened as she read the titles. Pressing the print key she printed copies of the articles and then closed her search window. Folding the articles in half she tucked them under her arm and set off to find the books on her hand written list. Twenty minutes later she had located three books that promised detailed information on shape shifters and folk lore surrounding such legendary creatures.

Satisfied that she had found good source material on shape shifters, Jessica headed to the children's reading room to find Jason. Red-headed twin boys were seated at a media table watching a classic Disney movie from the 1960's. Periodic giggling emitted from the pair as a group of runners sped around a running track on the screen.

"Go Godolphin!" one of the boys suddenly erupted, unaware that with the headphones on he was speaking much louder than librarians tend to like. Jessica glanced over at the screen and saw one of the runners stop and look at what he thought was a relay baton only to find a hot dog in his hand. More giggles erupted from the twins.

Quickly looking around the room Jessica was unable to locate her brother. She looked behind bookcases and tables and even searched through a pile of bean bag chairs in the corner. No Jason. Leaving the reading room she went over to the librarian's desk to speak with the lady behind the counter.

"Excuse me ma'am," Jessica began politely.

"Yes?"

"I came in here with my little brother."

"Ah yes, I remember the two of you. He is a little cutie."

Jessica fought back the urge to roll her eyes at the idea that her little brother was a cutie. Instead she smiled and asked, "He didn't leave the library did he?"

"No, I would have noticed. He spent some time in the children's reading room, and then asked me for bigger books on snakes. I took him to the adult section dealing with zoology."

"Zoology?"

"The study of animals," the librarian responded. "Would you like me to show you where it is?"

"Yes please," Jessica replied and then followed the librarian down several rows of books.

As they arrived at the section on zoology Jessica could easily see that Jason was not there.

"He is probably wandering down the rows of books," Jessica said to the librarian. "Thank you for helping me. I am sure I will find him around here someplace. I'll keep looking."

Jessica began searching up and down aisle upon aisle of book shelves. The more looking she did the more she became concerned that something had happened to Jason. With each passing second the eerie feeling that Jason was in trouble grew stronger in her mind.

"Help me Jessica."

Spinning around Jessica expected to see her brother. All that met her eyes was a section of biographies.

"Jason where are you?"

"Help me." Jason's voice was clear as a bell.

Quickly searching the rows of books around her she began to think she was losing her mind.

"That's it," she muttered to herself. "His voice is in my mind."

Concentrating hard on her little brother she could clearly hear his voice in her head.

"Where are you?" she thought.

"Up here," Jason's voice came back.

Looking up Jessica saw nothing but the ceiling.

"A lot of good that does me," she thought. She blinked her eyes. Had she just imagined it, or was the ceiling sparkling? Rubbing her eyes she looked up again. The sparkling on the ceiling was clearer now and it took the form of a line. Her eyes began to trace the path of the line, and as she did the first spot of sparkling disappeared. Somehow the sparkling ceiling was leading her someplace.

"Hold on Jason," she thought strongly. "I'm coming to you."

"Hurry," his voice came back. "I don't know how long I can hang on."

Jessica hurried down a row of shelves watching the sparkles move along the ceiling. As she reached the end of the row the sparkles turned right and lead her down an aisle along the end of several bookcases, and then it stopped in the corner of the building.

"Where to now?" Jessica asked softly as the sparkles disappeared from the ceiling. She began looking around for a sparkling trail but no sparkles met her eyes. Then out of the corner of her eye she spotted something. The walls of the old library were covered with wood panels and molding. The wood of the panels had been stripped of all paint to show the beauty of the grain. There in the grain of the wood she saw what appeared to be a hawk in mid-flight and dangling from its talons was a snake.

"Could it be?" Jessica mused and reached out to touch the image. As she pressed her fingers against the cool wood panel she felt the wood give slightly and she heard a soft click. As she pulled back her hand the wood panel popped out slightly. "A hidden door. How cool is that?"

Gently pulling on the panel Jessica found it opened up to reveal a small, dimly lit room. Glancing down at the floor just inside the room she saw several small shoe prints that she was sure would match Jason's shoes. Slipping into the room she could hear a soft voice calling in the distance.

"Help me Jessica. I'm stuck and I can't hold on much longer."

15

I Scream, You Scream

"W"here are you?" Jessica thought once again.

"Up!" came the reply in her mind and also softly to her ears. "Now hurry!"

As her eyes adjusted to the dim light she spotted a circular wrought iron staircase. Grabbing the curving rail she began to ascend the staircase. It was hard to tell just how far the stairs would go but she knew she had to hurry. The stairs were remarkably stable despite their age and Jessica felt secure in climbing the structure. The tower felt dirty and it smelled stuffy and old. Several times she felt cobwebs brush across her face, and once the webs hit her in the mouth when it was open causing her to spit out fragments of web. The urgency of reaching her brother outweighed any feeling of repulsion from the dirt and grime surrounding her. Even her usual fear of spiders was overcome by the greater fear of her brother getting seriously hurt.

"Hurry Jess, hurry!" Jason's voice grew clearer and clearer to Jessica's ears, slowly matching the voice she still heard in her head.

Finally the steps ended at a wooden platform and Jessica squinted in the dim light trying to make out her surroundings and hopefully find her brother.

"Watch out Jess, the floor is bad," Jason said meekly. Looking down Jessica spotted her little brother desperately holding on to a post that supported the hand rail that bordered the platform. Only Jason's upper body was visible above the platform. Two floor boards had broken away and he had slipped through the hole. Jessica dropped to her knees at the top of the landing and grabbed Jason's wrist.

"Hang on," she told her brother. "I'll get you."

Reaching into the hole Jessica grabbed onto the back of Jason's shorts and began pulling. After what seemed an eternity of struggling, but in reality was less than a minute, Jason found that he was seated next to his new hero clinging to her tightly.

"Thank you, thank you, thank you," Jason panted. "I was almost a big splat spot at the bottom of the stairs. If you hadn't heard me screaming I would be dead."

"That's just it Jace," Jessica explained. "I didn't hear you screaming. I heard you in my head."

"You what?"

"I heard you in my head. I was concentrating on you and asking where you were and you answered in my head."

Jason sat and stared at his sister like she was crazy for a moment and then a look of understanding spread across his face.

"Of course," he said in awe. "Now that I think about it I heard you in my head too. It gives you the willies doesn't it?"

"It's because we are true Willies," Jessica reasoned as Jason nodded knowingly.

"What were you doing up here anyway?"

"I was wandering around the library and I bumped into the wall and it broke. Well it didn't break, but I thought it did at first. It turned out it was a..."

"Secret door. Yeah, I know."

"Oh right. Well when I saw the stairs I figured it was the tower I had seen from outside. I wanted to see what there was to see from the top. So I climbed up the stairs."

"And almost took the quick way back down."

"Yep," he said meekly as he looked down through the broken boards to the darkness below.

"Did you at least see anything interesting?"

"Oh yeah, you can see half the town from up here."

"Show me," Jessica urged her brother. "But let's be careful."

The siblings carefully stood up and Jessica prodded the floor boards with her foot.

"It seems like you found the only rotten boards up here."

"We need to be careful not to fall through them," Jason said confidently.

"You think?" his sister teased.

"If you look over here there is a window," Jason pointed behind his sister.

In her rush to free her brother she hadn't noticed that there were windows facing out from the tower. The window panes had heavy coats of dust and cobwebs on them but she could see spots where Jason had brushed away enough grime to see out. Peering through one such spot Jessica scanned the view. The old window pane was wavy and distorted but she could see the tops of buildings and houses down the side street next to the library. Wiping a larger area to look through Jessica could see to the edge of town in the direction where their house was.

"It's the giants," Jessica said to her brother.

"Giants?"

"You know Jason, Mrs. Murphy's giants. Those big redwoods that guard the path to her house."

"Let me see," Jason said as he crowded his sister at the window.

Jessica moved aside and began wiping another spot her brother had started and looked through the glass. The view was similar to the first but showed more of the down town area. There were a few people strolling along the sidewalks and she could even see a group of children playing in the park at the center of town. Squinting through the window she thought she recognized the group from her school.

"Probably Missy Brandt and her group of stuck up brats," Jessica muttered to herself as she moved on to the fourth window. She carefully avoided the hole in the floor as she moved around the platform and more than once grabbed the hand rail as an added precaution. Once again she expanded the area Jason had crudely wiped earlier. This view showed the street directly in front of the library. She had an eagle's eye view of everything happening on the street below. The hairstylist that their mother went to was locking up her shop. She could see their car parked between an antique car with over-sized fenders and what her grandfather called running boards down the sides, and a yellow slug bug.

Jessica looked down the street a little and saw the front of the copy shop. Two copy machines were in the front window but her mother wasn't at either of them. Next to the copy shop was an alley and she thought she saw some movement there. Craning her neck to get a better look at the alley she suddenly gasped.

"What's up?" Jason asked.

"I think it's a Fallen!" Jessica said excitedly. "I only saw it for a moment but I am pretty sure there is one in the alley across the street."

"Let me see, let me see," Jason said trying to push his sister aside. Jessica moved to make room for her brother and quickly rubbed the spot on the window widening the viewing area so they could both see out.

"It was behind that crate on the right side of the alley. I think it was looking down the street and then it went behind the crate."

The siblings peered intently at the entrance to the alley watching for more activity. For a while nothing happened and the children fell silent. The only sound that could be heard in the tower was the gentle creaking common with old buildings. Jason stood on his tip-toes to get a better look and suddenly he broke the silence.

"Ears!" he cried out. "I just saw an ear sticking out from the side of the crate."

"Are you sure?"

"Sure I'm sure. I know an ear when I see one."

"Ok, I see it now. And there is its head."

The Fallen slowly raised its head above the crate and peered down the sidewalk. The children turned their gaze to see what the Fallen was watching. Coming down the street was a girl about Jessica's age. She swung her golden hair back and forth as she walked along the sidewalk. A stranger seeing her on the street would come to the conclusion that this young girl was someone of importance, or at least acted like she was. Jessica knew her all too well and bristled at her egotistical manner.

"Missy," Jessica snarled.

"Is that the girl who…"

"Yes. Prissy Missy. Ew, she makes my blood boil!"

Jason began to giggle, "You sounded just like Mom."

"Well she just makes me, makes me," Jessica searched for the words that could express how she felt.

"Mad?" Jason offered.

"Yes!" she said in exasperation. Again Jason's giggle filled the air and realizing how silly she sounded had to join in with her brother.

The siblings continued to watch as Missy strutted her way up the street. Expecting to see the Fallen shrink down behind the crate as the girl neared the alleyway Jessica and Jason were surprised to see the creature climb on top of the crate. It slinked to edge of the wooden box, then placing a tentacle onto a downspout of the building next to the crate it leaned forward to peer around the corner. Missy was less than ten feet from the alley and the creature didn't shirk back and disappear as expected.

"You don't think it's going to," Jason began.

"Attack her?" Jessica completed his thought.

"Uh huh," he replied in a near whisper.

Jessica held her breath as Missy took the last few steps toward the entrance to the alleyway. Missy reached the edge of the alleyway and appeared to be mere inches away from the repulsive little creature. Though the Fallen should have been clearly visible to the young girl, she seemed to be oblivious to its presence. Surprising the children even more than the lack of reaction to the creature by Missy, was the fact that she stopped walking. She stopped dead in her tracks right next to the red-skinned little creature. Jessica gasped loudly as the Fallen extended a tentacle towards Missy's head. The end of the tentacle brushed Missy's ear and the girl looked around to see what had touched her. She appeared to be completely blinded to the hideous little beast now touching her.

Jessica began franticly trying to find a way to open the window she was looking through. No matter what a horrible girl Missy could be at times, she didn't deserve to be attacked by a beast like a Fallen.

"I've got to warn her," she said in desperation. But her actions came too late. The beast now had both tentacles wrapped around Missy's neck. It leaned its head towards the side of her neck and bared its vicious looking fangs. Jessica could no longer bear to look at the attack taking place on the street below.

16

We All Scream for Ice Cream

J essica crouched down on the platform high in the library's tower. She buried her face in her hands and cringed as she pictured the terrifying things the beastly Fallen must be doing to Missy on the street below.

"So weird," Jason said in awe.

"Spare me the details and just tell me when it's over," his sister said as she fought back tears. If Jessica had not known about boys, and their fascination with all things gross and disgusting, she would have been sickened by his lingering at the tower window.

"Well I think it's kinda over," he said.

Whether it was the brevity of the activity, or that the carnage didn't match what passes for entertainment in movies or television, Jessica couldn't help but notice that her brother sounded disappointed. Standing again she kept her hands in front of her face to avoid seeing the gruesome scene through the window.

"How bad is it?"

"It's actually not bad at all. Just plain weird."

"Weird? As in, it sure is weird to see blood all over the place? Or weird like the Fallen did a tap dance on Missy's skull as he ate her face off?"

Jason started laughing at his sister's question. Jessica took her hands from her face and shoved her brother lightly on the shoulder.

"Knock it off. This is serious."

"Well Missy didn't think so," Jason countered.

Jessica turned to the window and saw Missy crossing the street apparently heading to the ice cream parlor.

"She's alive?"

"Don't sound so disappointed Jess. Maybe you will luck out and she will get hit by a bus before she makes it to the other side of the street," he giggled.

"Really funny squirt," Jessica said as she rubbed her knuckles against the top of her brother's head. "I think we've seen enough for now. We had better get our stuff and check out. Mom won't like it if we are late showing up especially since we are so filthy."

Jason gazed down at his clothing, and in the dim light could see a layer of dust all over. Brushing himself off a bit he looked up at his sister.

"Think Mom will notice?"

"It's Mom. She would notice if you had a slight smudge underneath your shoe," Jessica responded with a smile as she directed her brother back down the circular stair case. The trip down seemed much quicker than it did going up and soon the duo were at the base of the stairs looking for the latch to open the secret panel.

"We ought to try and sneak out of the tower without anyone noticing us," Jessica said in a hushed voice.

"Why is that?" Jason whispered.

"There might not be many people who know about this secret door. It may come in handy sometime and the fewer people that know about it the better. Does that make any sense to you?"

"No, yeah, well…yeah, yeah it does. Kind of like not telling anyone about the Fallen. It means a lot less splaining."

"X," Jessica corrected her brother. "It means a lot less explaining."

"Yeah, like I said. A lot less splaining."

"Oh brother," she sighed in exasperation.

Easing the secret panel slowly open a crack Jessica peered cautiously through the opening. When she felt confident nobody could see them she pulled the panel open and slipped back into the library. Jason followed close behind his sister. Jessica paused behind a row of book shelves and examined her little brother. For all the activity he had just been through, and the filth in that tower, he was remarkably clean. She brushed some dust from his shorts and had him turn around as she searched for other signs that they hadn't just been checking out books. Perusing her clothing she found there was very little dirt to be brushed off. Even the cobwebs she knew she had gone through while climbing the stairs were now gone.

Jessica went to the shelf where she had left her books and gathered them up. Turning to her brother she said in low tones, "Where are your books?"

Jason nodded for her to follow him and he head down an aisle and then turned right at the next opening in the bookcases. Turning left down that row he continued to the next opening and turned left again. Then he turned left and headed back to where they had made their first turn moments before.

"Are you lost?" Jessica asked her brother as she recognized having just been by the same row of books.

"Nope," Jason replied.

As he turned to follow the same route again Jessica grabbed him by his shoulder, "Listen squirt we don't have time for your games. Where are your books?"

"This is how I went before," Jason explained. "The only way I can remember where my books are is to follow the path backwards from the secret door."

"And so you kept going around in circles?"

"Only three times," he said looking up at his sister with big doe eyes.

"Knock it off Jace and skip the second and third trips around the mulberry bush will ya?"

"If we are going around the mulberry bush that would make you a monkey wouldn't it?" he said with a twinkle in his eye. Before Jessica could smack him on the back of the head, Jason skipped quickly down the row of books and stopped at the opening he had turned left before to circle around.

"Found 'em," he said taking three books off the shelf. Then he hurried to the front desk hoping to keep far enough in front of his sister to avoid her wrath.

Fighting back the urge to get back at her brother for wasting her time Jessica shrugged her shoulders, let out a long sigh and took her books up to the front desk where she waited for her brother to finish checking out his books.

"Field Guide to Snakes in California," the librarian listed his books, "Stories and Myths of Snakes and other Creatures, and Danny and the Dinosaur."

"Danny and the Dinosaur?" Jessica asked.

"I have to have one fun book," Jason defended his choice as he gathered his books.

"Yeah, but you have read that book dozens of times. I bet you have it memorized."

"Don't knock the classics."

"Now who is sounding like Mom?" Jessica said with a giggle. Looking up at the clock on the wall she saw that it was 8:25. "We need to get a move on. We have five minutes until we meet Mom."

The children finished their business at the front desk of the library and headed out the ornate front doors and down the granite steps of the library. Watching for oncoming traffic, the pair crossed the street and made their way to the ice cream parlor. As they reached the entrance they smelled a hint of sulfur.

"Smell that?" Jessica asked her brother as they paused outside of the ice cream parlor.

"The Fallen," her brother confirmed. "Do you see it?"

"No, do you?"

"Nope."

The siblings looked inside the window and saw no sign of the little creature. Also missing from view was their mother. Jessica spied Missy Brandt at the counter paying for ice cream. Looking down the street towards the copy shop she still saw no sign of her mother.

"Mom should be coming soon," she reassured her brother. "Let's just wait outside for her."

"Ok," Jason agreed as they sat on the wrought iron bench in front of the ice cream parlor.

A moment later they heard the bell on the door next to the bench ring. Missy Brandt exited the shop carrying a waffle cone with large scoops of ice cream covered in colorful sprinkles. At first it seemed she was going to walk away without acknowledging the siblings, then she turned to look at Jessica and Jason.

"Well look who's here," Missy said with a distinct tone of superiority. "Jessica Cow-well and her little brother."

The way Missy drew out the first syllable of Cowell always grated on Jessica. She knew it was meant to irritate her but Jessica had long ago determined she wasn't going to let the snobbish girl get to her.

"It's Cowell," Jason corrected Missy. Jessica shot an elbow into Jason's ribs in an effort to keep him quiet. It had the reverse effect when Jason exclaimed, "Ow!"

"Hello Missy," Jessica said politely. "How is your summer going?"

"It's busy, busy, busy," was the haughty reply. "If I'm not at a swim party I'm having friends over for slumber parties."

"That's nice," Jessica replied curtly.

"Close, personal friends," Missy emphasized.

"Of course."

"Have you heard the latest?"

"The latest what?" Jessica responded patiently and noticed the smell of sulfur was increasing.

"The latest information silly," Missy said tossing her hair back like she had seen older girls do in efforts to draw attention to their selves. In doing so Jessica caught a glimpse of the fallen. It had transformed into snake form and appeared to be clinging to Missy's back and had its head near her ear. Jessica let out a small gasp but covered it over with a forced cough.

"Information about what?"

"About that awful witch."

"What witch?" Jessica asked.

"That witch that lives at Redwood Glen. You must have heard about her."

"She's not a witch…" Jason said in defense of Mrs. Murphy.

"There's no witch at Redwood Glen," Jessica confirmed and then watched as the Fallen appeared to whisper in Missy's ear.

"There is too," Missy said. "She's been killing animals out in the forest. And then she turns their bones into magic potions."

"That's a lie!" Jason shouted at Missy.

"Is not!" Missy shot back.

Jessica settled her brother down. Seething inside about the accusations about her new friend she maintained her composure and asked, "Where did you hear such silly rumors?"

"They are not rumors."

"Well if they aren't rumors where did you get your information?"

"I heard it from, from…" Missy paused mystified. The Fallen whispered in her ear and Jessica strained to hear what the red snake was saying. "I heard it from a very reliable source," she finally said confidently.

"Well it sounds like you don't even know who you got your information from. Rumors and gossip are nothing but bad news. You should really be sure of your information before you start spreading lies around," Jessica said emphatically while trying to avoid lecturing Missy.

"Well I…" Missy searched for the proper words to say. This time the Fallen did not prompt the girl on what to say. "I don't have to take this from you."

With a flip of her hair Missy stormed off down the street. In her anger she had clenched her fists and in doing so had crushed her waffle cone causing the ice cream to ooze all over her hand. Disgusted with the mess she flung the ice cream and cone remnants into the gutter. The Fallen dropped off her back and slithered into the gutter to greedily eat the ice cream. As Missy disappeared around the corner the Fallen looked up to notice Jessica and Jason watching it. Hissing at the children it turned and disappeared into a nearby grate that lead into the storm drain system.

"I would say that is one of Missy's close, personal friends," Jessica quipped.

"I don't know who is worser, Missy or the Fallen."

"Worse," Jessica corrected her brother. "I'd say it's a close call."

"What's a close call?"

The children jumped as they heard the voice of their Mother.

"What?" Jessica muttered.

"You were saying it's a close call. And I asked what is a close call."

"Oh," Jessica responded as she tried to think. "It's a close call between whether I'm going to have peanut butter cup or fudge ripple ice cream."

"How about you Jason?"

"Bubble gum all the way," Jason said cheerily.

"How come I could have guessed that," Wendy said with a grin. "Come on kids, let's get some ice cream."

17

Discoveries and Deliveries

By the time the children and their mother arrived home it was too late for anything except baths, brushing teeth and heading to bed. Wendy busied herself in the kitchen sorting through her copied papers and arranging them into groups. Jason went in to kiss his mother good night before heading to bed.

"Night Mom," he said sleepily as he gave his Mom a kiss on the cheek.

"Did you brush well?"

"Yep," he said half-heartedly.

"Let me see," Wendy said.

Jason reluctantly opened his mouth for his mother's inspection.

"Did you even brush?" she asked her son.

"I'm too tired," Jason moaned.

"Upstairs Mister and brush your teeth," Wendy said firmly while displaying her characteristic smile.

Jason trudged back upstairs to brush as Jessica was coming down stairs to say goodnight.

"I told you she would notice Jace," Jessica said in passing.

"Yeah, yeah, yeah," Jason mumbled.

Jessica entered the kitchen and gazed over the stacks of papers laid out on the table.

"Need any help Mom?"

"Oh thank you honey for offering. I think I just need to plow through this on my own. I have an idea of how I want it organized. Once I have it lined up in a logical order it should come together pretty quickly."

"Ok. Well you know where to find me if you need any help," Jessica offered.

"I certainly do. You will be up in your bed asleep," Wendy said as she winked at her eldest.

"I was hoping to do a little reading before going to sleep."

"Reading eh? Did you pick up something interesting at the library tonight?"

"I think so," Jessica admitted. "I thought I would at least thumb through a few pages and see what it is like."

"Ok," Wendy consented. "But don't stay up too late. I know you are on vacation but you still need…"

"I know," Jessica interjected. "I still need a good night's sleep because I am still growing."

"Am I that predictable?" her mother asked.

"Only when you are being motherly," Jessica chided. Hugging her Mother around the shoulders and kissing her cheek the young girl bounced out of the room and up the stairs.

Snuggling into bed she grabbed a book off her nightstand and withdrew the papers she had printed at the library. Jessica shuffled through the papers until she came to the one that interested her most. It contained an old newspaper article from the local paper. The title of the article stated "Murphy Dismissed by School Board". Jessica slowly read the article and then reread it again. According to the article Mrs. Murphy had been dismissed from her teaching job about twenty-five years earlier for behavior the school board felt was "unstable and detrimental to the safety and security of the students". The article cited several incidents where Mrs. Murphy had claimed there were dangerous snakes and other creatures loose on the school grounds and in some of the buildings. All searches for the animals turned up nothing.

Accompanying the article was a photograph of Mrs. Murphy appearing at the school board hearing. Though she looked younger than the woman Jessica knew from her afternoon at her house in the glen, in some ways the person in the picture looked more tired and worn out. The caption of the photograph described the scene by saying, "Popular teacher Murphy leaves school board meeting surrounded by upset supporters." A group of serious looking men sat at a table in the background of the photograph and Jessica correctly surmised that these were the school board members. She knew she had seen some of them around town, though they naturally looked much older than they did in the photograph. As she was about to return the article to the stack of papers on her nightstand something caught her eye. One of the children following Mrs. Murphy out of the board room looked a lot like Jessica herself. Taking a closer look she suddenly giggled.

"It's Mom," she couldn't help but say out loud. So often she was told how much she looked like her mother and here was an example before her very eyes. Jessica studied her mother in the photograph a few more minutes and determined that she was a couple a couple of years younger than the girl she saw in the picture.

Putting the article away Jessica then chose a book she had checked out on shape shifters. She began eagerly reading the book but the activities of the day soon caught up with her and she succumbed to the power of sleep. Her dreams were a mixture of the adventures in the library's tower, her dealings with Missy, and images of what it must have been like to be in school with Mrs. Murphy as her teacher.

Finally her dreams drifted to Mrs. Murphy at her home. Jessica and Jason were walking down the path towards the cottage in the woods when they saw Mrs. Murphy step out on her porch and wave at the children. Jessica smiled as Jason waved back. Her smile only lasted for a moment as they saw a Fallen appear on the porch roof above Mrs. Murphy. Jessica felt frozen in mid-step as the Fallen swung down off the edge of the roof and flung itself at Mrs. Murphy's face. Jessica tried to run toward Mrs. Murphy but her feet seemed tied in place. As Mrs. Murphy tried to defend herself against the vicious little creature three more scampered out from under the porch and began assisting their fellow Fallen. Jessica looked to Jason in the hopes he could assist their new friend. Jason was busy trying to fend off the pointy headed Fallen who was scratching up his legs. Reaching down to free her own legs she found a group of Fallen gathered around her trying to pull her to the ground.

When Jessica awoke she was flailing her feet which were tangled up in her sheets. "Get off me!" she said in a panic believing she was still fighting off Fallen. As her mind cleared, and she realized she had been dreaming, she fell back onto the bed and gave a big sigh of relief. Staring at the ceiling she reflected on the final portion of her dreams. It was so vivid and terrifying. Jessica felt her stomach knotting up as she thought about the attack. Releasing her feet from the tangled sheets Jessica swung her legs out of bed and quickly dressed for the day.

In the hallway outside of her room she was nearly knocked over by her brother who was up uncharacteristically early.

"Watch out Jace," Jessica exclaimed.

"We've got to get to Mrs. Murphy's house," her brother responded breathlessly.

"I was thinking the same thing," Jessica responded. "I had a dream she was…"

"Being attacked," Jason interrupted. "I know. I dreamed she was being attacked too."

"Where was she attacked in your dream?"

"You and I were on our way to her house and she came out on her porch," Jason explained.

"And a Fallen swung down from her roof?"

"Bingo!"

"Ok. Let's get going," Jessica said as they headed down the stairs.

As the pair reached the kitchen they were stopped by their mother.

"What are you two up so early about?" Wendy said as the children stopped in their tracks.

"Uh, we wanted to get an early hike in," Jessica claimed.

"We want to head up by the pond," Jason added.

"Before you two go out you need to get some breakfast."

"But Mom," Jason complained.

"No buts about it. Sit and eat," their mother insisted.

Reluctantly the siblings sat at the table as their mother got out some dry cereal and bowls. As Wendy retrieved spoons and milk the children filled their bowls.

"Mom, do you remember having Mrs. Murphy for a teacher?" Jessica asked cautiously.

"Mrs. Murphy? How do you know about Mrs. Murphy? She was my teacher a long time ago."

"Oh Jason and I met her on a hike."

"Oh that's right. She used to live up beyond the pond. I remember how magical her house seemed to me as a child. How is she doing?"

"Well she was doing fine last time we saw her," Jason answered. "We're just not so sure..." His response was interrupted by a sharp kick to the shin from his sister. Rather than complaining he realized his sister was right in stopping him.

"She said to say hi to you by the way," Jessica quickly added. "So what was she like as a teacher?"

"Well Mrs. Murphy had a way of teaching that just drew you right in to the subject. I think she was probably the best teacher I ever had. Each day in her classroom was a new adventure.

117

The reason I still love to learn things is because of her. I have always thought of her as a wonderful woman too. There were quite a few students, parents and even teachers who felt the school really suffered after she stopped teaching."

"What happened?" Jessica inquired. "Why did she stop?"

"Well as I recall Principal Brandt never seemed to like Mrs. Murphy. Somehow he convinced the school board that she was a dangerous influence on the students and even made claims that she was mentally unbalanced," Wendy said thoughtfully with a faraway look in her eyes as if she were reliving the days of school life with Mrs. Murphy.

"Principal Brandt? Is he related to Missy Brandt?"

"I think she is his granddaughter. Principal Brandt's son was a year ahead of me in school and as I recall he told the school board a lot of lies about Mrs. Murphy. In fact he called her a… That's not important now."

"He called her what?" Jessica pressed her Mother.

"He said very mean things that weren't true," Wendy replied as her expression saddened.

"I bet he called her a witch," Jason said angrily.

"Jason!" Jessica exclaimed.

"It is a horrible word to call anyone Jason. But you are right. That is what he called her."

"But she isn't a witch Mom. Mrs. Murphy is a really nice lady," Jason reassured his mother.

"She certainly is," Wendy agreed. "She is a wonderful woman and I owe her so much for all she taught me."

"We want to go visit her this morning. Would that be alright?" Jessica asked.

"I think that would be a wonderful idea," Wendy said as a smile returned to her face. "In fact I was up all night working on my papers and I baked some cookies while I was at it. Why don't you take a dozen of them up to her house?"

"Thanks Mom," Jason said hugging his Mom.

"We'd like that. We will be sure to tell her hello from you."

"Let her know I will be up to visit her soon," Wendy said as she began placing cookies in a plastic container. "But before I go anyplace I am going to take a nap."

"Okay Mom," Jessica said as she began cleaning her spot at the table. "We should be back by noon. We'll be quiet when we get back."

"Thanks honey," Wendy said sweetly before heading to her room. "You two be safe, and remember your manners around Mrs. Murphy."

With their mother off to bed, the siblings quickly finished cleaning up after their breakfast and readied themselves for the hike to Mrs. Murphy's house. Packing the cookies and water bottles in a backpack the pair were soon locking the back door and heading across the lawn on their way to Mrs. Murphy's house. As the pair wound their way through the path to the dirt road they quickly related identical stories about what they had dreamed during the night. Memories of seeing Mrs. Murphy attacked by the horrible little Fallen spurred the children to hurry along the road at a rapid walking pace.

18

Showdown in the Glen

After sharing their dreams the pair continued up the dirt road in silence. The distance to Wexler's Pond was quickly covered, though it seemed longer than it should to the siblings due to their desire to get to Mrs. Murphy's house as quickly as possible. Arriving at the pond Jessica became aware that all she could hear was the slight panting of herself and her brother.

"Do you hear it?" Jessica said as she paused by the edge of the pond.

"Hear what? I don't hear anything."

"That's what I mean," Jessica whispered. "Listen closely."

Jason paused and concentrated on listening to his surroundings.

"I don't hear it," Jason finally said. "What do you hear?"

"That's just it," Jessica said softly. "There are no sounds. No birds, no bugs, nothing."

Suddenly the absence of noise hit Jason. His jaw dropped as he took another opportunity to listen to the world around him. His eyes scanned the trees and bushes for life. The only movement he noticed was the jet stream trailing behind a very distant airplane likely on its way from one of the airports in the bay area.

"Not even a breeze to listen to," Jason said in awe. "What do you think it means?"

"I don't know," Jessica replied unable to mask the tone of concern in her voice. "I know it's supposed to get really quiet before an earthquake. But I wonder if it has something to do…"

"With the Fallen?"

"Yes."

"We had better hurry," Jason said as he turned to continue the trek to Mrs. Murphy's house.

"Wait," Jessica responded as she placed her hand on her brother's shoulder to stop him. "We need to be smart about this. We need to be careful as we go. If Mrs. Murphy has been attacked we won't be able to help her if we get attacked too."

"So what do we do?"

"Look for any signs of the Fallen. Snake trails, little foot prints like we saw before that they make. Don't rush into anyplace without knowing what is going on there. And I think we might need to find weapons."

"Weapons?"

"Big sticks or something. Keep your eyes out for a branch you can use like a club."

"Okay," Jason said as they began moving up the road scanning the ground and watching the underbrush for signs of the Fallen. As they neared the bend in the road Jason found a sturdy branch that resembled a long baseball bat. Pulling off a few small clusters of leaves attached to the branch he swung it through the air.

"Looks like a good club Jace," Jessica said admiringly then gently teased her brother. "Just be careful who you hit with that will you?"

Jason chuckled at his sister's comment and shook his branch at her playfully. "Just don't make me mad."

The pair continued up the road and began spotting tracks that resembled the hoof marks they had seen before that they knew were made by the Fallen. There were multiple sets of tracks and the children could see variations indicating there were at least four different creatures that had been there. The tracks appeared to come out of the woods on one side of the road and disappeared into the woods on the opposite side of the road.

"They are headed to Mrs. Murphy's house," Jessica said in a low voice.

"Let's hurry," Jason said eagerly.

"Let's be careful," Jessica cautioned.

The children continued cautiously along the road to the point where they had been surprised by Mrs. Murphy their first time up the path. Jessica paused and looked off into the brush along the pathway. Moving near a bush she knelt down and reached under the prickly branches.

"What is it?" Jason whispered.

Holding up an axe handle she turned to her brother, "I think you dropped something when we were here before."

Jason blushed as he realized how his fear of being captured by who he thought was a witch had caused him to lose his weapon.

"Well I was scared."

"I'm not blaming you. I was scared too. In fact I don't even remember what I did with my broom handle. Do you want to keep the branch or do you want the axe handle?"

"I'll keep the branch."

Jessica swung the axe handle through the air a few times and looked at her brother, "Don't worry Jace, I have pretty good aim."

"Just remember I am on your side."

The children moved carefully down the narrowing trail towards the Giants. Watching the trees and bushes carefully they made their way to the huge redwoods that marked the hidden trail to Mrs. Murphy's house. Reaching the trees Jason admiringly patted the craggy bark of the one giant as he looked up at the massive redwood.

"I will go first and go to where the flowers start," Jessica whispered to her brother. "Don't come through the trees until you hear me tap on the tree three times. That way if the Fallen try to attack in these trees we both won't get caught."

"Why can't I go first?"

"Because I'm older and I said so."

"But."

"No buts," Jessica insisted, sounding quite a lot like their mother. "And I need you to promise me something."

"What is that?"

"If I tell you to run, don't hesitate, you just run. You run home and get help from Mom. Got it?"

"Got it."

"Pinky swear?" Jessica pressed.

"Pinky swear," Jason said extending his pinky finger to hook it with his sister's pinky finger. "Do you think we ought to do something like pray first?"

Jessica looked at her younger brother and choked back a tear, "I've been praying ever since waking up from that horrible dream."

Jason nodded and then bent his head and prayed silently as his sister patted his shoulder and slipped between the giant redwood sentinels. Lifting his head again he looked around at the bushes and trees around him. Everything around him was as silent as it had been at Wexler's Pond. Even though the distance from the giant redwoods to the flower blanketed clearing was just a few feet, it seemed like an eternity to the young boy as he waited for his sister's signal.

Jason involuntarily jumped when the first tap sounded through the trees. It was a soft sound yet solid and distinctly that of wood against wood. Two more taps came and Jason began creeping through the trees and down the pathway towards the clearing. He slipped up behind his sister who was crouching behind a bush scanning the clearing.

"See anything?" he whispered.

Jessica shook her head in reply then turning to her brother she whispered, "If Mrs. Murphy is okay she is going to wonder why we are sneaking around her property. But if she is hurt or is about to be hurt we have to worry about the Fallen because they could be anywhere. I'm not sure what we should do."

"Well we could run as fast as we can to her house."

"That could scare Mrs. Murphy. I guess maybe we should just walk right up the path. We need to keep our eyes and ears on everything around us."

"Okay. Should we leave our sticks here?"

"No. Let's use them like they are walking sticks. That way if there is nothing wrong we won't look too strange. But if there is trouble we will be ready for it."

Jessica slowly stood up and scanned the field of wildflowers before her. Despite the vivid blossoms of the flowers the entire field seemed bleak and dreary. At first the young girl felt that perhaps there was a storm cloud overhead casting the area into shadow. A quick glance at the sky proved to her that was not the case. The children moved slowly yet steadily up the pathway towards the plant covered cabin in the clearing.

Out of the corner of his eye Jason thought he saw some movement to his right in a patch of California Poppies. The flowers moved gently as if pushed by a breeze but Jason could feel no wind at all.

"I think we aren't alone," he whispered to his sister.

"I am getting that idea too. And I don't think it is Moustache."

Instinctively the pair gripped their sticks tighter and moved more cautiously, if a bit quicker, towards the house. The children froze as they noticed the front door opening at the front of the cabin. Jessica raised her axe handle a bit in readiness and held her breath as the door stopped moving. There was a slight rustling sound from the cabin and suddenly Mrs. Murphy appeared in the door frame.

Relaxing at the sight of their new friend the children began hurrying towards the cabin. Mrs. Murphy stepped out onto the porch and walked to the edge as they had seen her do in their dreams. Both children felt compelled to look at the roof of the porch to see if there was a Fallen looming overhead. Jason let loose an audible sigh of relief. The elderly lady waved to the children and smiled as they approached.

Jason broke into a run towards the front porch of the cabin as his sister continued to scan their surroundings. Jessica turned to look at her brother when he suddenly froze in place.

"Jason?" she called to her brother and then ran to catch up with him. "What is it?"

Jason began lifting his club and positioned it as if he were a baseball player preparing for a pitch. Jessica furtively searched for what had caused the sudden change in her brother. Believing he had spotted a Fallen hidden in the flowers or near the cabin Jessica realized what had put her brother on guard. Mrs. Murphy set her eyes on the young boy and Jessica fixed her eyes on Mrs. Murphy's eyes. They were solid black and completely void of the warmth and caring they knew the old lady possessed. The young girl was certain that the woman she saw before her could not be Mrs. Murphy.

19

Attack of the Fallen

"How many do you think are here?" Jessica whispered to her brother as she furtively looked around the enclosed field of flowers.

"At least one pretending to be Mrs. Murphy. I think there might be another behind the listening bench."

"I think we need to be ready for more than that. Remember what I said about running if I tell you to run?"

"Yep," Jason whispered solemnly. "The only way I am running is if you are running with me."

"I appreciate that. But if you feel you need to run just run. And one other thing."

"What's that?"

"You know how Mom has tried to teach us not to fight or hurt someone else?"

"Yep."

"I don't think it applies to the Fallen. In fact be sure to hit 'em as hard as you can. Because I don't think they are going to play nice."

"Got it. By the way I think there are some Fallen behind us."

"You want the ones behind us or the fake Mrs. Murphy?" Jessica asked as she raised her axe handle. She too had caught sight of the hideous little creatures out of the corner of her eye. She had also become aware of several more Fallen creeping through the wildflowers nearby.

"I'll take the ones behind us," Jason said confidently. "Shouldn't we have something to say to start this off? I mean like charge, or Geromino or something?"

"It's Geronimo not Geromino."

"So is that what you want to say?"

"Nope. I think we should say 'Kick Butt'."

"Oooo, you're going to be in so much trouble with Mom for saying butt."

"Right now I wouldn't mind being in a bit of trouble with Mom."

"I know what you mean." Jason had to agree.

"Ready or not it's time to KICK BUTT!" Jessica ended up yelling.

"KICK BUTT!" Jason responded as he spun around to face the Fallen behind them.

The false Mrs. Murphy stepped off the porch. Her smile was quickly replaced with a vicious snarl of jagged teeth. As the Fallen version of Mrs. Murphy approached the children she suddenly collapsed into a pile of clothing and six fat red snakes slithered out from the pile.

"Take that!" Jason yelled as he swung his club at an approaching Fallen.

Jessica heard her brother's branch make contact with a solid object. The ear piercing shriek emitted by the creature raised goose bumps on the young girl's arms. She clenched her club tighter and started advancing on the six snakes. As she did, three of the Fallen appeared on her right and another two Fallen transformed from snakes and stepped out of the patch of bluebonnet wild flowers on her left.

She had just decided the three Fallen on her right posed the most immediate threat and needed to be dealt with first, when she felt a strong wind pushing down on her. Looking up she was startled to see several Red-Tailed Hawks sweeping down just over her head. The hawks flew low just above the trail and two of them grabbed a red snake in each talon then veered off about ten feet away before landing on the ground. A third hawk landed just behind the two remaining red snakes that had previously formed part of the imitation Mrs. Murphy.

"I think we have help Jace!"

"Good because there sure are a lot of Fallen," Jason's voice was a bit strained as he swung again at a snarling Fallen.

Jessica swung her club at the nearest Fallen who deftly ducked out of range of the blow. The creature's quick movement saved him from a solid blow but the creature just behind him was taken by surprise as the solid handle struck him soundly in the shoulder sending him reeling into a rose bush. The Fallen who had ducked lunged forward and began clawing at Jessica's leg. The girl tried to kick the creature free from her leg but he clung to her and tried to sink his fangs into her knee. Swinging the bat downward she caught the Fallen across his back causing him to fall away from her.

Glancing from her bloodied shin to where the hawks had landed she saw that six Fallen had transformed from snakes into the forms she had begun to associate with the hideous beings.

The hawks were nowhere to be seen. Instead of hawks there stood three boys who appeared to be in their early teens. Each had vivid red hair and their fair skin seemed to glow.

"I think those hawks are the Guardians," Jessica said trying to catch her breath.

"As long as they are here to help I don't care what they are," Jason said as he swung at, and missed, a bruised Fallen. "I would be glad to share some of these creatures with them."

Jessica hadn't noticed that the Fallen who had been on her left had crept up behind her, and she soon found herself trying to fight the creatures in two directions. Just as she would send one Fallen sprawling into the dirt she could sense another coming at her from behind. From what she could determine there was a growing number of Fallen and the battle seemed to be going in the favor of the red creatures.

Jason was out of breath and struggling as the tenacious creatures kept attacking him. Fewer of his swings with the branch found their targets and he was quickly losing strength. The two Fallen he was initially fighting had now been joined by three more. Just as he was about to give up hope two hawks swooped in behind his enemies and landed on the pathway. He marveled as the hawks transformed into young men who looked strikingly like the three Jessica had already spotted. The Fallen attacking Jason were unaware of the new arrivals and the two redheads motioned to him not to reveal their presence. Jason gritted his teeth with a new determination as he continued to swing his branch at the onslaught of attackers. The Guardians slipped up behind the group of Fallen and began grabbing the wiry creatures and assisting the struggling boy.

Several of the Fallen had taken up sticks and rocks to use as weapons against the children and Guardians, and the battle in the normally tranquil glen raged on. The air hung heavy with the rank odor of sulfur as several of the Fallen sought to escape from the fight by transforming back into snakes and disappearing into the flowery field. Jessica winced in pain as a rock hurled by one of her attackers found its mark on the back of her head. At the same time one of the Fallen attacked her already bloody shin which caused her knees to buckle. As she dropped to the ground she let out a scream as several of the creatures leaped on to her back and began pulling her hair and tearing at her arms.

Feeling overwhelmed by her attackers Jessica felt a sense of impending doom and frantically called to her brother, "Run Jason. Get out of here. Get to safety." Trying her best she tried to pry the creatures off of her but with each attempt she made, another creature scratched, bit or struck her. The weight of the creatures was too much for Jessica and she collapsed into the dirt as the creatures continued to claw at her. Fighting with all her might she managed to roll over onto her back so she was able to at least face her attackers.

Meanwhile Jason was having more luck than his sister due to the arrival of his redheaded allies. The fight was still an uphill struggle as each Guardian was dealing with at least four of the Fallen and Jason was still personally facing three of the creatures on his own. Using every ounce of strength he possessed the young boy swung his branch at a Fallen who was hitting him in the shoulder with the handle of a broom. The branch made direct contact with the head of the Fallen. The blow made a stomach churning sound as if a watermelon had been dropped onto a sidewalk splitting it open. Had the sound not come from the head of one of the enemy, Jason would have likely been sickened by the knowledge of the sound's source. As it was he managed a thin smile as he saw the Fallen sprawl head first into the path apparently knocked unconscious by the blow.

Jessica struggled with the mass of Fallen attacking her. Two of them had managed to wrench the axe handle from her hands and were jointly trying to wield the weapon. Few of their attempts at striking the girl were successful as they were inept at cooperating with each other. The other Fallen were better organized and worked together to pin Jessica's wrists to the ground by her side. One rather round and heavy Fallen sat on her ankles effectively restraining the girl to the ground. As she tried to lift her head several of the creatures grabbed her streaming hair and held her head firmly to the ground. A shadow spread across her face and she looked up to see what was blocking the sunlight. Hovering over her head she recognized the pointy headed Fallen. He held a rock, as large as he was, high over his head. His intent was clear in Jessica's mind. He meant to smash her head in with the weapon.

He hissed through jagged teeth as he poised the rock and Jessica was able to clearly make out what he was saying, "Die human!"

20

A Battle Won—A War Rages On

Anticipating the rock crushing down on her head at any moment Jessica squeezed her eyes closed in preparation for pain like she had never experienced before. More importantly she began praying. Instead of pain the girl felt nothing.

"Is that it?" she thought. "Have I been killed and it was so quick I didn't feel it?"

Suddenly the sounds of battle came to her ears once again. Knowing she didn't want to see the rock coming at her head Jessica refused to open her eyes. The pointy headed Fallen flexed his tentacle like arms and began the motion to crush the girl's head. He was stopped short by a swift kick to his chest. The unexpected blow sent him flying back into a clump of lilies with the large rock landing on his own head.

"As a friend of the Guardians, and ally of the King, I command you to release my daughter or taste my wrath!"

Jessica opened her eyes to see her mother standing by her side kicking another Fallen into a patch of gravel. Smiling weakly up at her mother Jessica twisted her wrists, freeing herself from the Fallen that were holding on to them. The Fallen pulling her hair continued holding on until Wendy grabbed one by the throat and lifted it off the ground.

"I said let her go!" she said punctuating each word by poking the beast in the chest.

The Fallen struggled in the grasp of the woman and then noticed a golden necklace about her neck. The creatures eyes widened and it began to shriek repeatedly. Rather than fight with the creature Wendy smiled slyly as she noticed what the Fallen's eyes had locked on and she brought an object attached to the gold chain to her lips. Jessica could just make out what looked like a gold conch shell pressed against her mother's lips. Once her mother had shown her all her jewelry and she could not remember ever seeing this piece before.

"I warned you," Wendy said and then blew in to the shell.

All the Fallen began to shriek and writhe in misery at the sound emitted by the shell. But the Guardians seemed to take great pleasure in the sound and were strengthened by the tones it created. Jason and Jessica found the sound to be beautiful and almost hypnotic. The Fallen ceased their attack and covered their ears as they cowered and shrieked even louder as if they could drown out the sound of the shell.

Jason looked around at the fear on the faces of the Fallen. Those Fallen who were not struggling with Guardians, or in the grasp of his own mother's hand, began running away or transforming into red snakes and disappearing into holes or beneath bushes. Realizing the enemies were on the run and escaping Jason pounced on the Fallen he had rendered unconscious and held on tight. One of the Guardians had produced some glowing cords and was binding the captured Fallen one by one. Once the creatures were bound in the cords they were unable to move, and apparently unable to transform into anything that could escape their bindings. Jason's captive was taken from him and trussed up as the others had been. The Guardian nearest him patted the boy on the back.

"Well done Jason," the Guardian told him. "You have the heart of a fierce warrior."

Jason couldn't help but smile at the compliment, "Thank you. You weren't so bad yourself."

Wendy handed her captured Fallen over to the Guardian binding the prisoners, then getting a good look at the Guardian she asked, "Phillip is that you?"

"Yes Wendy," the Guardian said with a smile.

"You haven't changed one bit," she said in amazement. "It has been decades since I saw you last."

"I've seen you quite a few times. You just haven't known it at the time. Remember we are always looking out for friends of the King. And you Willies are some of the King's best friends."

"Mom," Jessica said as a Guardian helped her to her feet. "You are a Willie?"

"Yes dear," her mother smiled at her. "I guess you and Jason take after your old mom don't you?"

"We sure do Mom," Jason said as he hugged his mom around her waist.

"Mrs. Murphy!" Jessica suddenly cried out as she recalled the whole reason for being in the flowered glen that morning. "I'm afraid she might be seriously hurt. We had this dream that she was attacked."

"I know," Wendy said with a note of concern in her voice. "When I laid down to nap after you left this morning I had a dream about her being attacked and you and Jason being here and in danger."

While one of the Guardians took control of the prisoners, the rest joined the children and their mother in searching for the elder Willie. While Jason and several of the Guardians began searching through the lush garden one of the redheaded Guardians transformed into a red-tailed hawk and took to the skies for an aerial view of the surroundings. Jessica, Wendy and Phillip cautiously entered the cabin looking for the missing woman.

The room that had been so tidy on her previous visit was now a scene of turmoil. A broken wooden chair lay in a heap in the middle of the room. Shelves once neatly arranged with antiques and knick knacks were now just heaps of objects on the floor. Wendy began searching the kitchen as Phillip entered the bedroom. Jessica opted for going down a small hallway that led to the bathroom. Pictures had been pulled off the wall and lay strewn down the hall. Reaching the bathroom door she had to push several times to open it. A cabinet had been tipped over blocking the door from opening properly and from what she could see the bathroom had been ransacked like the rest of the house.

"Mom come quickly!" Jessica cried out as she saw Mrs. Murphy slumped over in the bathtub. Desperately pushing her way past the cabinet the young girl knelt beside the tub.

"Mrs. Murphy, it's me, Jessica," the girl said tenderly as she took the wrinkled hand of the woman in hers. It was still warm and she heard a low moan coming from Mrs. Murphy. Hearing a slight commotion behind her Jessica turned her head and saw

Phillip standing in the doorway, the cabinet was back in place and the room had been returned to a clean and orderly state as Mrs. Murphy would normally keep it. Wendy came down the hall behind Phillip and as she reached the doorway he stepped aside to let her through.

Wendy knelt beside her daughter and began checking the old woman for injuries.

"Her pulse is weak but it seems to be getting steadier," Wendy said in an attempt to reassure her daughter. There were multiple claw marks on the woman's ankles and arms. As Wendy tenderly tilted the woman's head to the side she revealed a raised lump on her forehead with a two inch cut in the middle of it. "Jessica get a wash cloth and soak it in cold water then ring it out for me."

Before Jessica could move Phillip was handing Wendy a moist wash cloth.

"What took you so long Phillip?" Wendy said wryly. Pressing the cloth against the woman's forehead Wendy tenderly cleaned the cut. Phillip handed her another moist cloth which she placed around Mrs. Murphy's neck. The cool, damp cloth caused the woman to stir and soon her eyes fluttered open. Jessica held her breath as she was still half expecting to see hollow black eyes. Instead she saw the pale blue eyes of the sweet lady she had met the other day.

"Are you okay Mrs. Murphy?" Jessica eagerly asked.

Mrs. Murphy blinked a few times as she adjusted to her surroundings. Her face lit up as she looked at Jessica.

"Jessica my dear," she said weakly. "You came back to visit me. How wonderful. Did you bring your brother?"

"Yes Mrs. Murphy. And my mother is here too."

"Your mother? Wendy?" Mrs. Murphy glanced beside Jessica and gasped in astonishment. "Wendy Thomas. What a delight to see you again."

"It's Wendy Cowell now Mrs. Murphy. I'm afraid the Fallen have really injured you."

"Oh those nasty little creatures. They caught me by surprise just after breakfast. Can you please help me out of this tub? We will be much more comfortable in the other room."

"I think we need to get you some medical attention Mrs. Murphy," Wendy said emphatically. "You've got a nasty cut on your head and perhaps other injuries. My car is on the dirt road near the giants. I can get you to the hospital in no time."

"Why whatever for Wendy?" Mrs. Murphy said in astonishment. "Have you forgotten that you are a Willie?"

Wendy looked stunned for a moment at the old woman's response and then a look of revelation came across her face. Softly she placed her fingers on the lump on Mrs. Murphy's forehead. After a few seconds she removed her hand and the lump and cut were completely gone. In amazement Jessica blinked a few times and still saw no cut or swelling. When she looked at the woman's other wounds they too were missing.

"Once a Willie," the old woman said softly.

"Always a Willie," Wendy responded as she and Jessica helped Mrs. Murphy to her feet.

Upon returning to the living room they found everything had been returned to where Jessica remembered it had been during her first visit. Jason and two of the Guardians were just entering the cabin as Mrs. Murphy was encouraging everyone to take a seat.

"Mrs. Murphy!" the young boy called out as he ran to her throwing his arms around her in a big hug. "You are alright! I was so worried."

"Oh, my sweet Jason. I am alright thanks to your mother. She has always had a very special gift of making people feel better. I was just about to tell how the Fallen attacked me this morning."

The old woman and Jason took seats next to each other on an antique couch and Mrs. Murphy continued her story.

"I had just finished cleaning up after breakfast when I looked out the window and saw Jessica and Jason coming up the pathway. I went out on the porch and was waving to them when one of those nasty little creatures climbed off the porch roof and attacked me. Then more of the Fallen were rushing at me and I called to the children for help. That is when I noticed their eyes."

"It wasn't us was it Mrs. Murphy?" Jason asked.

"No it wasn't my dear. As you probably guessed it was the Fallen pretending to be the two of you."

"Just like they pretended to be you when they attacked us," Jessica relayed.

"I am just so glad you decided to visit me when you did," Mrs. Murphy said appreciatively.

"Well we all had a dream you were in trouble," Wendy said. "There was no way we could stay away."

"What was that thing you blew into Mom?" Jessica asked her mother, her eyes fixed on the gold shell.

Lifting up the shell Wendy smiled at her daughter. "That is a story for another day Jessica. It is quite a story, isn't it Phillip?"

Phillip smiled and for a moment the children could sense that this Guardian was far older than any of them could imagine.

"It is quite a story my friend, one of many. And I know that Agatha has quite a few stories to tell herself," the Guardian added.

"Agatha?" Jason queried.

"Mrs. Murphy," Phillip replied. "Agatha Murphy has been a friend of ours since she was about your age Jason. I am sure you will hear many of the stories your Mom and Agatha have to share. And I have no doubt you will have plenty stories of your own to share with future generations of Willies."

The conversation was interrupted as one of the Guardians entered the cabin and approached Phillip.

"Captain, the prisoners have been transported and the area has been cleaned and secured."

"Very good. Post double sentries," Phillip said with a very official tone. Turning to the Cowell family and Mrs. Murphy he added, "I must go report to my superiors. Rest assured we are never far off, and friends of the king will always have our help."

"It was good seeing you again Phillip. Thank you for protecting my children," Wendy said appreciatively.

"It is always good seeing you. You have raised your children well Wendy," he said as he exited the cabin. The children ran to the door to wave good bye just in time to see several red-tailed hawks taking flight. They watched as the hawks disappeared over the tree tops.

"Are you sure we can't take you to the doctor for an exam?" the children heard their mother ask the elderly woman.

"My dear you still have your gift and I am feeling better than I have in years," Agatha Murphy replied. "It is such a treat to see you again."

After a brief visit the Cowell family was finally on the pathway back towards the towering redwood giants. There were no longer any signs of the battle they had experienced. Even where the pointy headed Fallen was crushed under the rock had been returned to how it looked just before the fight.

"I can hardly wait for the next Willies adventure," Jason said excitedly.

"It will come all too soon I'm sure," Wendy said with a heavy sigh.

"I hope so," Jessica added, her eyes dancing in anticipation.

As the trio disappeared between the giants they were unaware of the activity forty feet above them in the branches of the giant redwoods.

"They are the ones my liege," a fat red snake hissed as it clung to a branch swaying in the breeze.

From the branches of the neighboring redwood a sinister voice replied, "Keep me posted on their every movement scum. You know the fate that awaits you if you fail me."

A bony hand reached across to touch the tip of the red snake's tail. With a single touch the end of the snake shriveled and flaked off as the snake winced and fought back the urge to cry out from the pain.

"The kingdom will be mine," the sinister voice added as the pair watched the Cowell family get into the family car, "no matter the cost. It will be mine."

ABOUT THE AUTHOR

C.S. Curtis lives in a small Northern California community, surrounded by a menagerie of animals, with his wonderful wife and three of their four sons. Their oldest son is married and lives nearby. Even his children will admit that their Dad has a dark and warped sense of humor. Having previously served as a youth pastor, teacher (from Middle School to College age students), juvenile detention officer and a host of other things in between he has found his calling in exploring his imagination through writing.

www.ingramcontent.com/pod-product-compliance
Lightning Source LLC
Chambersburg PA
CBHW030612130626
46552CB00002B/532